the
**far cry**

Other titles available in Vintage Crime/Black Lizard

By Fredric Brown
**His Name Was Death**

By David Goodis
**Black Friday**
**The Burglar**
**Nightfall**
**Shoot the Piano Player**
**Street of No Return**

By Richard Neely
**Shattered**

By Jim Thompson
**After Dark, My Sweet**
**The Getaway**
**The Grifters**
**A Hell of a Woman**
**The Killer Inside Me**
**Nothing More Than Murder**
**Pop. 1280**

By Charles Willeford
**The Burnt Orange Heresy**
**Cockfighter**
**Pick-Up**

By Charles Williams
**The Hot Spot**

the
# far cry

fredric brown

VINTAGE CRIME / **BLACK LIZARD**

vintage books • a division of random house, inc. • new york

First Vintage Crime/Black Lizard Edition, July 1991

Library of Congress Cataloging-in-Publication Data
Brown, Fredric, 1906–1972.
The far cry / Fredric Brown.
p.   cm. —(Vintage crime/Black Lizard)
ISBN 0-679-73469-4
I. Title.   II. Series: Vintage Crime/Black Lizard.
PS3503.R8135F37   1991
813'.54—dc20       90-50591   CIP

Manufactured in the United States of America
10  9  8  7  6  5  4  3  2  1

the
**far cry**

*S*udden terror in her eyes, Jenny backed away from the knife, her hand groping behind her for the knob of the kitchen door. She was too frightened to scream and anyway there was no one to hear, no one but the man who came toward her with the knife— and he was mad, he must be mad. Her hand found the knob and turned it; the door swung outward into the night and she whirled through it, running. Death ran after her.

Eight years passed.

Then:

What happened started quite casually, as most things do. It started on the eighteenth of May, a Thursday.

There was a man named George Weaver who had just taken a room at La Fonda, a hotel in Taos, New Mexico. He had just finished shaving; he was wiping the residue of lather from his face with the moistened end of a towel when the phone rang. He hung the towel over the edge of the washbowl and went out to the hotel room to answer the phone. "Hello," he said.

"George Weaver?" The voice was familiar but he couldn't place it. He said, "Yes, this is Weaver."

"This is Luke, George. Luke Ashley."

Weaver's face lighted up. "The hell it is! What are you doing in Taos? How'd you know *I* was here? Where are you?"

The telephone chuckled. "Which question do I answer first?"

"Where are you?"

"At the hotel desk downstairs."

"Then the other questions can wait. Come on up, Luke."

Weaver cradled the phone, then opened the door of his room and left it ajar while he went back into the bathroom and finished drying his face. A chance to see Luke Ashley was both pleasant and unexpected. He hadn't seen Luke in—it must be over two years now.

Looking at his face in the bathroom mirror, Weaver wondered how much change Luke would see in it. The last few months had been pretty hard on that face; they'd done things to it—and it hadn't been much of a face to begin with. Always a little thin, it looked gaunt now and the eyes had a haunted look.

He heard Ashley come in and met him halfway across the room. "Luke, old boy. How in *hell* did you know I was here? I didn't know I was stopping over here myself until I checked in an hour ago. Intended to drive on through to Santa Fe."

Ashley was tall, thin, balding; he looked a bit like William Gillette as Sherlock Holmes—a very appropriate resemblance, Weaver had often thought, for a writer of true crime stories for the fact detective magazines. And Ashley sometimes humorously capitalized on it. As now, he said:

"Elementary, my dear Weaver. I saw your car parked outside—a green Chevvie coupe with a Missouri license." Ashley sprawled himself into an easy chair and threw his long legs over the arm of it. "Put on a shirt, George, and we'll go down and have a drink somewhere."

"But how did you—? That car's only a year old, Luke, and you never saw it. How'd you know what kind of car I had?"

Ashley sighed. "All right, if we must get down to mundane facts. I'm on my way to the coast—L. A.—and I routed myself through Kansas City so I could stop over a few hours to see you. You'd left only a day ahead of me and Vi told me you were heading for Santa Fe and what route you planned to take. She described your car and gave me the license number in case I caught up with you, so I've been watching for it. When I got to Taos just now, I drove once around the plaza and there you were parked in front of the hotel here. So I came in and asked the clerk if they had any George Weavers on hand, and they did."

Weaver nodded, "You must really have been highballing to catch up to me when I had a full day's start. Well, not too much, maybe; I've been taking my time driving, watching the scenery and not pushing too many hours a day. I've got orders not to be in a hurry about anything. I—I suppose Vi told you about that?"

"A little. I didn't talk to her very long. What are your plans, George?"

Weaver had taken a sport shirt from the suitcase open on the bed and had put it on. Now, buttoning it, he walked over to the window and stood looking out. He said, "Look at those God damned beautiful mountains. I could look at them all summer—and maybe I will. I *was* heading for Santa Fe, but now I don't know if I'll go the last seventy miles or not. Hell, it's five years now since I lived there and I don't know whether I want to see the people I used to know then or not. Haven't kept up correspondence with any of them. Vi keeps up correspondence with Madge Burke there, the girl who used to work in the restaurant with her, but that's about our only contact.

"I like this place, Luke. Partly because I don't know anybody here, partly because it's smaller than Santa Fe and more peaceful. Besides, it's got something; I don't know what. I feel better already, I think. Anyway, I'm going to stay here at least long enough to look around. If I find a place I'd like to live in, at a price that I can afford, I'll stay all summer."

Ashley nodded. "Taos is a good little town. Beautiful summer climate—it's even better than Santa Fe in the summer. Same altitude, seven thousand. Winters are colder than Santa Fe, I'm told, but that isn't a factor if you're not staying that long anyway. And it's an artists' colony, which means there are interesting people to meet if you get tired of being a hermit and want company."

"You sound as though you know the place pretty well, Luke."

"Just from having spent a week or so here three summers ago. I was writing up the Manby murder case. That was a screwy deal if there ever was one. Know anything about it?"

Weaver shook his head.

"You'll probably hear about it if you stay here; it's a local legend. And there was another pretty good murder case here seven—no, eight years ago. Girl named Jenny Ames. I tried to get enough dope to write that one up too, while I was working on Manby, but I couldn't get enough solid facts to make a good story out of it. And they never caught the killer anyway, and that's a bad angle for a fact crime story."

Weaver said, "I think I remember the name. That would have been while I was living in Santa Fe, and I think I read something about it in the papers. What are you working on now, Luke?"

"Put your shirt tail in and I'll tell you over a drink. Or leave your shirt tail out—nobody in Taos will care."

Weaver put it in. They went down to the plaza and wandered around it and into El Patio; they had cool, tinkling Tom Collinses under a huge sunshade in the open air.

Luke Ashley took a deep breath. "It *is* nice here, George. I'd forgotten what it's like to breathe this air. It's mañana country, and picturesque as hell. Those blanket Indians you see on the plaza, they're not Chamber of Commerce window dressing. There's a thousand-Indian pueblo a couple miles from town and that's the way they really live and dress. And if you get to know any of the Taos Indians, you'll like them; they're real people."

"You haven't told me yet what you're doing, Luke. Why the trip to Los Angeles and what will you be doing there and for how long?"

"Just hadn't got around to telling you; didn't mean to be mysterious about it. Regal Pictures is making a documentary on the big-shot gangsters of the Prohibition era in Chicago, centering around the Valentine Day massacre there. I've done a lot of writing about those days and they hired me as technical adviser. It's a three-month contract so I'm driving out in order to have my car to get around in while I'm there. Left Chicago three days ago and I'm due in L. A. in three more. That's all about me.

"Now how about you, George? Vi told me you were coming out here for the summer and that she would join you later, but she—uh—"

"Acted a little funny about it?"

"Well, I wouldn't say that— Oh, hell, she *did* act a little funny about it. If you don't mind telling me, what's the score?"

Weaver made wet circles on the table with the bottom of

his glass. He saw from the whiteness of his knuckles that his hand was clenched too tightly around the drink, and he made his fingers relax.

He said, "A little case of overwork, Luke, that's all. They called it a breakdown. I was in a sanatorium for six weeks. I'd been working too hard and all of a sudden I hit the ceiling and came apart.

"The stay at the san got me over the worst of it, but the doc said I'd better get away from work and spend the summer somewhere trying not to think about—" He managed a grin. "—about whatever business it was that I was in back in Kansas City. I'm supposed to forget it completely, so how can I talk about it? If you happen to remember what business I was in, don't mention real estate to me."

"Real estate? You mean that stuff about land and buildings?"

Weaver pretended to shudder. "Maybe that was it. Anyway, I'm ordered to paint pictures or write poetry or something, for the summer. To get away from everything and into something else. Three months at least, maybe longer. To do anything that interests me—doesn't matter much what—as long as I don't make any money at it."

"Listen, George, with this legal contract, I'm pretty solvent. If I can lend you some dough—"

"Thanks a lot, Luke. But I think I'll get by. I had some pretty stiff losses back in Kansas City—worrying about them and trying to make up for them is part of what started my breakdown—but I cashed out a few thousand bucks—enough to get by on for the summer, even for the fall if I stay that long, and still have a few bucks left to start myself in business again when I've got myself completely straightened out. I sold out my business so I wouldn't have to think about it, but it won't take much capital to get started again. That's one good thing about real estate—if you know the game and know the town you're operating in, and I know Kansas City inside out, all you need to start out is enough dough to rent an office and finance yourself a little while. You get listings and take a cut on selling property that doesn't belong to you."

Ashley nodded. "Well, if you run short I can spare some.

How long is Vi staying in K. C., before she comes out to join you?"

"She's coming in two or three weeks. We're sending the girls to a summer camp back in the Ozarks—the same one Ellen went to last year, and this year Betty is old enough to go too. But the camp doesn't open until the first of June so Vi is sticking it out back there till she can get the girls into the camp. She'll join me after that."

"How old are your girls now, George?"

"Ellen's six and a half. Betty'll be five in two weeks—just the minimum age the camp will take. They're good kids. Drive me crazy when I'm around them, but I miss them already."

"Do you good to be away from them, though. If peace and quiet is what the doctor ordered—"

"It is. Peace and quiet and anything non-commercial I can get myself interested in. And the girls won't mind being in camp. Anyway, Ellen won't—she was crazy about the place last summer, and I guess Betty'll like it too. And they'll be better off in camp than—"

He broke off, realizing what he'd been about to say. You don't tell even your closest friend that your children might be better off getting away from their mother for a while—and it was probably an exaggeration anyway; Vi wasn't that bad.

If Ashley guessed, he didn't ask. He said, "Something's happened to our drinks. Mice, maybe?"

"Could be. Should we have another?"

Ashley looked at his watch. "Maybe we should eat. It's only noon, but I've been driving since six-thirty on a light breakfast. Are you hungry?"

"No—but my appetite's been off. I didn't have any breakfast but coffee this morning, so I should probably try to put something down."

"Let's go, then. There used to be a place here—up the street toward the post office—called La Doña Luz. Wonderful grub. Duncan Hines rating. Run by a guy called Frenchy. If it's still here—"

It was still there. They ate mountain trout and Weaver found he had an appetite after all. It was the best meal he'd eaten in a long time.

La Doña Luz had a bar but they walked back to El Patio so they could have their after-lunch drink in the open air again. It was that kind of weather.

They talked about old times together—pleasant, casual conversation. Nothing sinister, nothing sinister at all. Just times they'd gone fishing together, poker games they'd played in, a couple of hunting trips they'd shared—all over two leisurely drinks in the leisurely sunshine.

After a little while Weaver said, "Let's take a drive around. I want a closer look at those mountains. I'll do the driving if you're tired. And, by the way, I'm getting more and more sure that I want to stay here for the summer if I can find a place."

"Okay, let's go. And I'm rested up now, so I'll drive. Let's take my buggy; it's a convertible and I've got the top down."

Ashley drove. Through Arroyo Seco and toward the mountains, along a road that got rougher the farther they went. After a while Ashley waved a hand toward an adobe house set back about twenty yards from the road, the first house they'd seen in about an eighth of a mile. He said, "That's where Jenny Ames got it."

"Who?"

"Jenny Ames. I mentioned her before. Victim in the murder case I couldn't get enough data on. Wasted two days before I saw I wasn't getting anywhere and gave up. But I got a good price for the Manby story so my stay here paid off."

They were past the house by then. Weaver had looked at it back over his shoulder until a turn in the road cut off his view.

"Nice place for a murder," he said. "Plenty isolated."

"Yes, plenty. It's the last house back on this road, nothing between it and the mountains. The road peters out from here; we won't be able to go much farther." He slowed down and pointed to his left. "The girl ran away from the house, back that way toward the foothills; took the murderer—what the hell was his name?—almost a quarter of a mile to catch her."

The road got worse. Ashley decided they'd better turn

around and did so at the first wide place he came to.

Weaver asked, "Anybody living there now?"

"Where? Oh, you mean the murder place? It looked deserted when we passed it just now. Nobody was living there three years ago when I tried to write up the story. Up to that time nobody'd lived there since the murder."

"Supposed to be haunted or something?"

"Not that I heard of. Don't know why it would be since the murder itself happened so far away from the building. No, I think the main reason is that it's a little too far from town for most people. And it wouldn't be much good for year-round living because the road gets pretty bad. And there are mostly Spanish people living out this way, and they wouldn't be interested because the land's no good and they want places they can farm, or at least have a garden. Land around there's just sand and sagebrush."

"But there must be a hell of a view from that place. How far is it from Taos?"

"Ummm—we came through Arroyo Seco and that's eight miles from Taos. I'd guess that house is another mile and a half or so. Say nine or ten miles from Taos. Why? You're not thinking of buying the place, are you?"

"No, not buying it. But if I could rent it for the summer, why not? There ought to be peace and quiet enough to last me the rest of my life, way out here. Know anything wrong with the idea?"

They were back at the place again and Ashley stopped the car. He looked dubiously across the creek at the house beyond. "Pretty primitive, pal. No plumbing: you'd have to carry water from the creek here—although that's only a few yards and the water's probably purer than you'd get out of a faucet. But there's electricity. And God knows there's isolation if that's what you want. Shall we go up and look at it closer?"

"Sure."

Ashley drove the convertible across the little wooden bridge that spanned the creek between the road and the house.

It was a three-room flat-roofed adobe building. Behind it, ten yards back, stood a rickety wooden outhouse and ten yards beyond that along the same path was a wooden shed. They walked around the house; its windows were boarded and both of the doors were locked.

"Good solid construction," Ashley said. "Cost a little to fix up, but not much. Labor's cheap here." He peered through a knothole in one of the boards across a window. "The furniture's still in there. Looks like the same stuff that was there when I was inside the place three years ago, which means it's the stuff Nelson left."

Weaver was staring up at the mountains. He asked, "Who's Nelson?"

"I remembered the name. The guy who killed Jenny Ames. Want to hear about it?"

"Not especially. Let's get back into town and find out who owns the place. If I could get it cheap enough— My God, look at that view, I could look at it all summer."

"All right, maybe you will. Come on."

They drove back to town and stopped at the Taos Inn, just before they would have reached the plaza. There was a patio there, too, and Ashley led Weaver to one of the tables. "Order yourself a drink," he said. "I'll go find out about that place for you. I'm going to see a guy called Doughbelly Price."

"You're kidding."

"I'm not. That's his name and he either handles or has a line on most of the property that's for sale or rent around here. And, at least three years ago, he had the handling of the Nelson place."

"But why should you do it, Luke? At least, why shouldn't I come along?"

"And talk about a forbidden subject? Nix, my friend, remember that you don't know what real estate is. Relax and wrap yourself around a cold drink while I find out the facts."

Weaver wrapped himself around a cold drink. In half an hour Ashley was back, grinning. "You got yourself a house," he said. "For free."

"What do you mean, for free?"

"Well, the next thing to it, anyway. Wait a second, I'll get us some coffee; I don't want another drink because I want to do some more driving. Or would you rather have another Tom?"

"Coffee sounds good."

Ashley went into the bar and then came back and sat down across from Weaver. "Coffee coming up. Okay, here's the deal on the house. Price says he's been trying to sell the place and that the house and four acres are listed with him at two thousand bucks—but it's been marked that for eight years and no takers. Furniture—he says it's not anything fancy, but that it's usable—goes with it. That's if you want to buy it, and I told him you didn't."

"Right," Weaver said. "Now get to the 'for free' business you were talking about."

"Price wants somebody to live there for a while to break the jinx, as he puts it. He'll let you have it for the summer if you'll fix it up and live there. He says he thinks the few repairs the house itself will need shouldn't run over about fifty bucks to get the place fixed up livably. That sounds pretty cheap but you can get labor out there for three bucks or so a day.

"He guesses it'll cost you another fifty to get the furniture fixed up, and that you'll probably want to add a few pieces if two of you will be living there and that'll run you another fifty or a hundred bucks—unless you want to get fancy about it. But he says if you improve the place that much you can live there this summer—or as late into the fall as you want to—for free. He says he probably wouldn't rent or sell it this summer anyway so he's got nothing to lose and with that improvement to the place, plus the fact that the jinx has been broken by somebody's living there, he'll have a better chance of selling or renting it next year."

The coffee came. Weaver sipped his, looking up at the bright blue sky over the rim of his cup.

Ashley said, "I told him you'd let him know by tomorrow."

"We can let him know today," Weaver said. "Maybe this Doughbelly Price—*is* there such a character, by the way, or are you kidding me?"

"It could happen only in Taos," Ashley said, "but there *is* such a character. And if you strain like that at a gnat, he has his office next to that of Jimmy Valentine, who is a public accountant. No, I'm not kidding you."

"All right, I'll believe you. What I started to say was that maybe this Doughbelly Price is crazy, but I'm not. I'm taking him up on that deal. As soon as we're through with this coffee."

"Good. I'll go around with you, and after that I'll have to push on. I want to get to L. A. as soon as I can and if I can put another couple of hundred miles behind me before I hole in for the night, I'll be that much closer."

Doughbelly Price was a little man in a big Stetson. He shook hands with Weaver and said, "Maybe I'm nuts for making you a deal like that, but I've been stuck with that joint for eight years. Maybe you can take the curse off of it."

Weaver grinned at him. "What do I sign?"

"What do you want to sign anything for? I couldn't read it anyway. Here's the keys. Go on out and fix it up and live there."

Weaver had himself a house.

He tried to talk Price into having a drink to seal the bargain, but Price said he had another appointment. He said, "Listen, Weaver, if you don't know nobody around here, you'll get yourself cheated less if you just get a contractor to do that fixing. Ellis DeLong, maybe. Unless you're a contractor yourself and know the local angles you ain't going to save yourself no money by hiring your own labor."

After they left Doughbelly Price's office Weaver had a little trouble persuading Luke Ashley to have one final drink for a stirrup cup before he left, but he finally prevailed. "All right," Luke said finally, "but better watch it yourself, George, in this altitude. Yes, you lived this high in Santa Fe, but not recently; you're used to Kansas City."

They had the final drink together in the little bar of La Doña Luz.

Ashley said, "Listen, George, I've got an idea. Living right there where the Jenny Ames murder happened, you might get a chance to dig in on it—and you might find it interesting to do the digging. If you do, and can round up enough facts to let me write the case up—after my three months in Hollywood—I'll cut you in on the deal. My by-line, of course, because that'll make it sell quicker, but I'll give you a cut of the check, half or more, depending on how much of the work is yours and how much is mine. And the true detectives are paying good rates right now. You might get enough out of it to cover what fixing that house up is going to cost you—and that would make your rent for the summer really for free."

"Nuts to Jenny Ames," Weaver said. "I'm out here to rest up, not to play detective on an eight-year-old murder case."

"All right, but sooner or later you'll get bored resting up—and the idea might sound better to you. If you change your mind before the summer's over, the deal stands. You might find it more interesting than you think. It was a Lonely Heart murder."

"What's a Lonely Heart murder?"

"That's one of the things you'll find out when you start digging in. Well, George, I've really got to go. It was swell seeing you again."

"Thanks for everything, Luke. And that was a good tag line you used just now; I *will* have to dig in enough to find out what the hell a Lonely Heart murder is. But no farther. I'm going to get myself some water colors and do some splashing around, and that's as hard as I intend to work."

When Ashley had left, Weaver found Ellis DeLong in the phone book and talked to him on the phone. He learned that DeLong's place was only half a block off the plaza and walked there.

He explained the deal he'd just made with Price.

"I know the house," DeLong said. "How much do you want done to it?"

"Whatever it needs—in reason. Mr. Price says fifty dollars ought to make it livable-in, outside of furniture. I'll double that if I have to, but I'd just as soon not. How soon can you get at it?"

"Tomorrow, I think. Work is slack right now. I'll send two men on the job and I doubt if it takes them more than a couple of days."

"That's fine," Weaver said. "Until I can get in the place I'm staying at La Fonda—you can get in touch with me there if anything comes up."

He went back to his room at the hotel and wrote a letter to Vi. Not a long letter, nor an affectionate one. They'd passed that stage long ago, shortly after the birth of Betty, almost five years ago. It was for the sake of Ellen and Betty—

He wrote:

Dear Vi,
  I've taken a place in Taos, a bit out of town but not too far; it's about twenty minutes' drive. It's a little primitive and isolated, but the scenery is marvelous— and it's a wonderful bargain for the summer. I hope you'll like it. [She probably wouldn't, he thought; but then again he wished she weren't coming.] You can reach me General Delivery in Taos to let me know when you'll arrive. The train doesn't come here, so buy your ticket to Santa Fe and I'll drive down there—it's seventy miles—and pick you up to save you the bus ride. Give my love to Ellen and Betty and tell them that their daddy . . .

He walked up to the post office to mail the letter and then back to the hotel. He didn't want another drink just yet; he wasn't hungry enough to eat; he didn't want to go back up to his room. Nor did he want to look for someone to talk to; he didn't quite know what he did want.

The sun was going down and the air was getting cool now.

He'd have to find something to do for the evening. There was only one movie in town, almost next door to his hotel, and only a Western was playing there. Occasionally, back home, he'd sit through a Western because Ellen was crazy about them (he sometimes called her Hopalong Weaver) but he certainly wasn't going to sit through one in any lesser cause.

Maybe reading would be the answer. He walked across the plaza to the drugstore and picked out a pocket book to read, a mystery.

He sat in the hotel lobby and tried to get interested in it, but it bored him. When he found that he'd read the same paragraph three times and still had got no meaning out of it, he put the book in his pocket and went out to walk. Maybe he could work up an appetite so he could eat and get eating over with; then he could go up to his room and stay there. Maybe, in pajamas and removed from the temptation to go out again, he could get interested in the book.

What, he wondered, was a Lonely Heart murder? Isn't every heart lonely, always?

Forget it. He walked.

After a while he found himself striding savagely across the evening. He forced himself to slow down.

The stars came out, and a bright moon, and a cool wind.

**I**n the morning it was raining hard. From his window Weaver could scarcely see across the plaza, let alone the distant mountains that had been so incredibly beautiful in sunlight. He closed the window and got back into bed, cursing himself for having got drunk the night before. Stinking drunk and on a solitary jag, sitting alone at a bar staring at his reflection in a blue-tinted backbar mirror, repelling with curt monosyllables the few who had tried to talk to him.

Why?

There was a bad taste in his mouth and he felt a great need for cold water. He went to the bathroom and drank two glasses of it. His hands were shaking so badly that he didn't care to risk shaving.

He knew he wouldn't be able to go back to sleep so he dressed, a bit fumblingly, and went downstairs to the coffee shop. The thought of food was abhorrent to him but he forced himself to eat some buttered toast with the two cups of coffee that he drank.

He felt a little better then, although his hand still trembled when he held it out and looked at it. (Making sure first, of course, that no one was watching him.) He'd either have to quit drinking so much or learn how to use an electric razor, much as he disliked one.

He solved the problem for the moment by getting shaved in the barbershop a few doors away. It was still raining moderately hard but portals made a porch-like roof over the sidewalks almost all the way around the plaza, so he didn't get wet.

The rain was a mere drizzle by the time he'd had his shave. He was able to walk to where he'd parked his car on a street off the plaza. He drove out the Denver road and turned off at the side road to Arroyo Seco. His Chevvie skidded dangerously and he saw that the road ahead was a sea of mud. He fought the skid and stopped the car slowly and carefully. He wondered if he should try to go on and remembered how much worse parts of the dirt road past Seco were than this section of it; surely they were impassable. Cautiously he backed out onto the asphalt main road and drove back to Taos. Living out there on a dirt road had been a mad idea. He'd go to DeLong and cancel the deal for fixing up the house, then give the keys back to Price. He hadn't as yet any investment—unless it was half a day's time—in the place.

DeLong was glad to see him. "A bit wet this morning," he said. "But I've got three men working on your place; they went out there early."

"You mean they made it over that road—or wasn't it so bad then?"

"Oh, it may be a little worse by now than it was earlier, but this is the first rain we've had in two weeks so it can't be so bad. You'll get used to a little mud once in a while—and it doesn't happen often."

"But—"

"I'm free now. Want to go out there with me and see how things are coming along? We can talk over any doubtful points—things we might not be sure whether you'd want done or not."

Weaver nodded. If things weren't too far along, if his investment wasn't too big, he could still cancel it. The rain had stopped.

DeLong's station wagon had no special tires but he made the road easily. He said, "We'll still have a few rains, but not many. Possibly for the next month there'll be about a day a week when the road will be a bit slippery and you'll have to drive slowly, but you can make it. There's a knack to driving in mud. And we'll have nine-tenths good weather from here on in; there's nothing to worry about."

The three men—one an Anglo, the other two Spanish-Americans—had knocked off for lunch when they got there. DeLong and the Anglo carpenter went over the place with Weaver, discussing what had been done and what should still be done. DeLong told Weaver, "Doughbelly's guess of fifty dollars wasn't bad. Not much material needed—a few new boards and nails, two panes of glass, some plaster patch. I think they can finish today and that about forty or forty-five dollars will cover it. Unless you want a fancy job."

"No, I don't want a fancy job," Weaver said.

The next day the sun was out and the road, although badly rutted, was almost dry.

The workmen had finished. Weaver looked over his domain and found it good—but greatly in need of cleaning. He drove the mile and a half back to Arroyo Seco in search of help. He inquired at the general store and was directed to a Spanish couple named Sanchez who were willing, for five dollars, to spend the afternoon cleaning. He drove them out to the house and left them there, after inventorying the furniture and other contents to decide what things he'd need right away. He drove into Taos and spent the afternoon picking up a few pieces of used furniture, some dishes and cooking implements and some bedding. He got back at five o'clock with all the smaller items in his car—two heavier pieces would be sent out by truck the next day.

The Sanchezes were just finishing. They'd done a good job and the place looked livable-in.

"I'll drive you back," he told them, "soon as I bring in the rest of the stuff from the car."

Sanchez gave him a hand with the carrying. He asked, "You buy this place, Mister Weaver? Or you just rent, huh?"

"Just renting. That is, I'm paying rent for the summer by getting the place fixed up."

"You live here alone, huh?"

Weaver explained that his wife would be joining him soon.

"Good." Sanchez nodded emphatically. "After what happened it would be bad to live alone here, Mister Weaver. My boy Pepe, he saw it, he saw the start of it."

"Saw—you mean he saw the murder?"

"Pepe, he saw him go for her, Mister Weaver, with the knife. Through that window Pepe saw it. He had been fishing up the arroyo—"

Weaver said, "Well, that's all the stuff out of the car. Come on; I'll take you home."

As the car crossed the little bridge and turned onto the road, Sanchez pointed back. "Right from here Pepe saw it, in that window, Pepe saw her back away to the door and the other after her with the knife, the man who lived here, Nelson. Then she got through the door and ran and Pepe could not see any more."

"He didn't try to help her, or get help?"

"Help her, Mister Weaver? Pepe he was only ten, only a boy. He came home and told me. I go to the store and talked on the telephone for the sheriff in Taos and he came, but I don't think he believed my Pepe. He went out to the house and he look around but find nobody home and no signs anything happen. He told Pepe that he see things. It was only when they find her body two months after back in the hills they know what Pepe told them was true."

After he'd taken the Sanchezes home, Weaver hesitated briefly deciding whether to return to Taos for the night or whether to pick up some groceries at the little store in Arroyo Seco and take them back to the house. Then he remembered that his clothes and toilet articles were still at the hotel and that, anyway, he was past check-out time at the hotel and wouldn't save any money by not staying there for the night. Besides, he had nothing to read, nothing to do at the house.

He moved the next day and laid in a supply of food. Not that he intended to do any great amount of cooking for himself; until Vi got there he'd have one meal a day in Taos, but he'd manage to make himself coffee in the morning and to fix himself some kind of a lunch. He laid in a stock of magazines and pocket books. He wanted to buy paints and paper but it was Sunday and he couldn't find any place open that sold artists' supplies.

The next day was beautiful again. Right after a late breakfast he drove into Taos and found a place called the Kiva where he could buy water colors and suitable paper. He intended to take literally the doctor's suggestion that he try painting; he'd never seriously tried it before but he had a knack for drawing and thought that with a little practice at handling colors he might not do too horribly.

He tried painting as soon as he got home and found that he enjoyed it, although it began to bore him after an hour or so. He read some, and he looked at the mountains. He even walked back toward them perhaps a quarter of a mile, and that made him think of Jenny Ames, one night eight years ago. This was how far from the house her body had been found—after a quarter-mile run through the night with a killer at her heels.

The night that followed was cool and, again, he couldn't seem to concentrate on reading. He drove into Seco and tried the tavern there. He was the only Anglo in the place and all the conversation was in Spanish. He was used to the sound of Spanish—he'd lived a long time in Santa Fe—but he'd never learned to speak it or understand it. That didn't matter tonight because he hadn't wanted to talk to anybody anyway. But there was something wrong with the atmosphere—or was he imagining a vague hostility that wasn't there? And he kept wondering whether they were talking about him—not that he cared if they did, but he couldn't help wondering.

After a while he bought a bottle from the backbar and drove home with it. He drank himself into a sullen stupor and went to bed, well before midnight.

In the morning he woke early and couldn't get back to sleep, although he felt lousy, too lousy even to make breakfast for himself. Was this what he'd come to Taos for? The doctor back home had made no objection to moderate and occasional drinking, but this made two nights out of five that he'd gone to bed drunk and that couldn't be good for him, physically or mentally. The doctor had told him that the heavy drinking that had preceded his breakdown had been a symptom and not a cause, but if he kept on—

He dressed and drove in to Taos—Seco is too small to have a restaurant—and the drive gave him enough appetite to enable him to eat a good breakfast and feel better.

At the post office there was a letter waiting from Vi:

> Dear Georgie—[He hated being called Georgie and had managed to break Vi of the habit of doing it verbally, but she still wrote to him that way whenever they were apart.]
>
> Im glad you found a place you like and hope your feeling good by now, I wish it had been Santa Fe because we both lived there and liked it once and had friends there, I guess it was mostly your friends but if Taos is what you want its all right by me, I dont know just yet what day I will come but it will be about a week yet and Ill write again and let you know in a few days, meanwhile the girls are fine . . .

She always wrote that way, one running sentence to a letter no matter how many subjects she covered, and she always left out the apostrophes in her contractions. Weaver had often thought that possibly they'd never have been married if they'd corresponded before the ceremony. Errors in grammar and spelling and punctuation always irritated him more than they really should; he knew that it amounted almost to a phobia with him, but he just couldn't help it. Vi hadn't had much education and she'd been working as a waitress when he'd met and married her, and there'd been nothing he could do about it. He'd tried at first to talk her into taking some classes at night school, but during the first year of their marriage it hadn't bothered him too much—there'd been passion as against grammar— and after the birth of Ellen he'd given up. Vi would always be ignorant and a little stupid—and basically, he'd decided, it was the stupidity that annoyed him more than the ignorance. Many poorly educated people have keen minds; some have that rarer quality, good taste. Vi had neither, and no amount of education would have given them to her.

He sighed, as he put the letter in his pocket, and wished again that she wasn't coming. But providing separate maintenance for the two of them for all summer, in addition to the cost of keeping the girls in camp, would be much more than he dared risk spending; he *had* to hang onto enough capital to finance a fresh start for himself in business in the fall. Now that he had acquired a place big enough for them both to live in—and had, in effect, paid his rent in advance for the summer, there wasn't any choice in the matter. Besides, they had already, before he'd left Kansas City, given notice on their flat for the first of June and had made arrangements to store the furniture. If Vi didn't come here, she'd have to stay at a hotel or rooming house; he'd have a hell of a time talking her into doing that, especially now that he'd already told her that he had a three-room place paid for, for the summer.

No, there wasn't any out, now.

The weather stayed bright and warm, except for the evenings, and the mountains stayed beautiful. No rainy, or even cloudy, days. Weaver painted, and the results weren't too bad, although his further efforts didn't seem to get any better than his first ones had been, and occasionally they were worse.

He read and walked and ate and slept and drank. Sometimes there was lonesomeness, but against it a strong basic urge to *be* alone that kept him from trying to make friends.

He didn't do too badly; he was drinking too much he knew, but at least he learned to avoid, for a while, doing any drinking till after dark. And he rationed his days to keep him going until then; after that there seemed nothing to do but try to read—sometimes he could concentrate enough to enjoy reading and sometimes he couldn't—and to drink until he got tired enough to enable him to sleep.

Whisky was getting to be a bit expensive, though, and he switched to wine, at least for the drinking he did at home. Prices of most things, he was learning, were higher in Taos or Seco than they'd been at home in Kansas City. Rent and clothes were all one could save on—clothes not because they cost less but because there was no need of wearing good ones; denim trousers and wool shirts were almost a costume. He'd been wondering whether to write to Vi again while he was waiting to hear from her, and finally decided to do so mostly to tell her to bring more of his old clothes along so he could save by wearing them out during the summer. And he told her not to spend too much for additions to her own wardrobe; she'd need cool things for the daytime and warm ones for the evenings, but they needn't be new or expensive things.

He found a practical use, finally, for the water colors; he composed a long letter to the girls that was only half writing, which Vi would read to them, and the other half little pictures in bright colors, of mountains and 'dobe houses and animals and Indians. They weren't good pictures, especially, but Ellen and Betty would get a big kick out of them and would think their father was a real artist.

The next day was a Sunday, and the post office wasn't open, nor were the taverns and liquor stores. It was a bad day; he slept till noon after having drunk too much once more and after having stared too much at the blackness through the windows until some small, and unremembered, hour of the night. He awoke needing a drink, and there was nothing left. He drove into Taos to get himself a drink to pick him up before he remembered the Sunday closing law. He drank a lot of coffee and it helped a little, but not much.

The sun was bright and beautiful as he drove back home but he saw the mountains and the scenery with a weary eye; he thought, the hell with it, what is scenery? It's like a book, possibly wonderful and magic the first time you read it, but can you keep on reading and rereading it indefinitely?

He tried to paint; he tried to read. Finally the day passed, and the evening, and he was able to go to sleep by midnight.

Monday was better. He woke without a hangover and at eight o'clock. He got his breakfast and wandered out into the bright morning, and things were good again.

But not too good. Sometime late this week or early next week Vi would be coming, and there are worse things than being bored or a little lonesome occasionally. The constant and unavoidable presence of someone who grates upon you is worse than solitude can ever be.

And aren't we all lonely, always? What the hell had Luke Ashley meant by a Lonely Heart murder?

He drove into Taos early in the afternoon because it was time for him to pick out and send a birthday present to Betty. He found a truly beautiful Indian doll that he knew she'd love; it cost about twice what he'd intended to spend, but he bought it and arranged to have it sent.

At the post office there were two letters for him, neither from Kansas City. One was from a friend in Santa Fe whom Luke Ashley also knew; Luke had given him Weaver's address. It suggested that he drive down for a week end there, even if he intended to spend the summer in Taos. Will Fulton. Weaver remembered Fulton too vaguely to want to spend a week end with him or even to drive seventy miles to see him.

The other letter was from Luke Ashley, on stationery of the Biltmore in Los Angeles. He stepped into the bar at La Doña Luz and ordered himself a drink before he opened it. He glanced again, first, at the letter from Will Fulton.

"It'd be hell, George, to have you so near and not get a chance to see you at all. Some of us might drive up but Luke didn't know just where you'd be living, so . . ."

Mentally, Weaver thanked Luke for that; Luke had recognized that he might not want to see anyone from Santa Fe.

"All the old gang will be glad . . ."

To hell with the old gang, he thought. He hadn't seen any of them for six years and he didn't want to now. He crumpled the Santa Fe letter and tossed it into the open fireplace. His drink came and he took a sip of it and then opened Luke's letter:

Hope you're not yet bored in your lonely retreat. I told a few people in Santa Fe—I stopped over there that night after I left you—that they could reach you through the Taos post office, but didn't tell them where you'd be living, so they wouldn't bother you in case you didn't want company. Or *are* you getting bored by now?

If you are, why not take my suggestion and do a little digging in on the Jenny Ames murder? There's even more reason for it now. I just got a letter from my best market telling me that they're starting a series of Lonely Heart murder cases—there have been quite a few of them—and the Jenny Ames deal would fit in beautifully.

If you can dig up enough data to let me do five thousand words on it, it'll pay three hundred bucks—extra for photographs, and you can at least take pictures of the place where it happened—and if you do all the leg work and I do all the writing I'll split even with you. Don't sneeze at a hundred and fifty bucks if it's something you can pick up in your spare time. And I know you're not supposed to work, so if this turns out to be work, drop it. You just might get interested in doing it and find out that it's fun instead. It wouldn't be for me, but then this is my racket and it's not yours and playing the other man's game turns out to be fun, while it's new, surprisingly often. Whenever you feel up to it, give it a whirl and see how it goes. If you can get enough dope at all, you should be able to do it in your spare time in a week. Don't forget the pictures—if you get enough good ones, that'll run your take up maybe another fifty bucks, which will be all yours. Picture of the house, one of the place where the girl was buried, maybe a picture of the boy who saw the start of the crime—those you can take yourself. Maybe you can dig up a picture of whoever was sheriff at that time and worked on the case. . . .

Weaver had another drink and thought it over.

Why not? he wondered. After all, a hundred and fifty bucks was nothing to be sneezed at if he could get it just for asking questions of a few people and forwarding the data to Luke. And he had a camera that was good enough to take the pictures that might run his share up to two hundred dollars; he'd forgotten to bring it with him to New Mexico but he could write Vi to bring it with her luggage. And he could tell her to bring his portable typewriter, too.

When he'd finished his drink he went back to the post

office and bought two airmail postcards. He used the desk there to address and write them, one to Vi telling her to bring the camera and the typewriter, one to Luke, "Okay, will do." He mailed them.

He felt more cheerful than he'd felt for several days. Investigating a murder—even an eight-year-old one—would give him something to do and might be interesting. And earning a hundred and fifty or two hundred dollars would definitely be a good idea, especially at something so far from his usual occupation that it could hardly be classed as work.

He celebrated his decision by having a good dinner in Taos.

It was getting dark when he got back into his car and drove toward Arroyo Seco.

Darker than he dreamed.

**H**e wasn't in any great hurry to get home, and, as he neared the little town, it came to him that there was no time like the present for starting what he'd decided to do. He stopped at the house of Mr. Sanchez.

Sanchez answered his knock at the door. When he saw who it was he smiled broadly and gestured with his hand. "Come in, Mister Weaver, come in, please."

Weaver went in. The place was smaller than his own but there were about a dozen children of all ages playing on the floor, doing homework at a table, three of them helping Mrs. Sanchez, who was washing dishes in a huge dishpan. But the room was amazingly quiet.

Twenty-four eyes, all of them dark, focused on Weaver, who stood uncomfortably, his hat in his hand, just inside the door.

Sanchez said, "Please to come this way, Mister Weaver." He led Weaver through a doorway to the right and into a small parlor, furnished with a splendor far beyond the room through which they had just passed. Weaver looked about him, torn between admiration and amusement. The room was spotless, but side by side with a beautiful example of native blanket weaving was a hideously gaudy pillow, "Souvenir from Denver." Next to a hand-carved santo that might have been a hundred or two hundred years in age sat a ceramic Donald Duck. Half of the furniture was locally handmade—the heavy, sturdy Spanish-American style that is so beautiful in its functional simplicity—and the other half was an assortment of cheap and flimsy mail-order stuff; from its placement there could be little doubt of which half the Sanchezes were most proud.

Weaver was motioned courteously to a fancy but uncomfortable-looking chair that was obviously in the mail-order category. "Please to sit down, Mister Weaver."

"Thanks." Weaver sat down a bit stiffly, wondering how to begin to explain his errand. None of the others had followed them into the parlor; he decided that the room must be a sanctum sanctorum, and probably for men only. But the door had been left open and, sanctum or not, wide eyes in the other room sought vantage points for staring in at him.

But none of the children in the other room, he had already decided, could be Pepe. Pepe, if he'd been ten years old eight years ago, would be eighteen now, and there had been no boy older than fourteen or fifteen.

Looking at the doorway, which he was facing, Weaver smiled at one little girl and she smiled back shyly. He felt more comfortable and less out of place after that. He nodded toward her and said, "I've got a little girl just about her age, and another a year and a half older."

"They come here with your wife, Mister Weaver?"

"Not this sunmmer. They'll be at a girls' camp back— East." It seemed strange to refer to Kansas as the East, but that's how Sanchez would think of it.

Sanchez nodded and said, "Yes, Mister Weaver," and then there was a moment's silence; Weaver realized that it was up to him to broach the object of his visit. No matter how long he waited, Sanchez would be too polite to ask. He cleared his throat and wondered where to start, and then realized that the simple truth was the best approach.

He told Sanchez that a writer friend of his had asked him to get details about the murder of Jenny Ames so he could write a story about it.

Sanchez nodded politely again. "You want to talk to Pepe then, huh? My boy who saw them? Pepe is at the dance. I will send Luis for him, Mister Weaver." He looked toward the doorway and spoke into the silence beyond it. "Luis, you will bring Pepe home. Quick."

The boy who looked to be about fourteen started toward the outer door.

Weaver said, "Wait, please," and as the boy paused, he tuned to Sanchez. "Please don't pull your son away from a dance, Mr. Sanchez. There's no hurry about this. I can talk to him tomorrow, any time."

Sanchez gestured deprecatingly. "It's not matter, Mister Weaver. The dance it is not for an hour yet. Pepe he left early. He watches the others play pool or maybe Pepe he plays himself. It will not hurt him to come. The poolroom and dance hall are very near. Five minutes it will take to come. Go now, Luis."

It was so definite that Weaver didn't protest further.

While they waited, Weaver said, "Of course I'd like to hear from your son just what he saw that night. But, even besides that, I'm really starting from the beginning. I don't even know yet who or what Jenny Ames was. Or anything about the man who killed her—except that his name was Nelson—or why he killed her. I'm sorry, but I'm afraid I wasn't interested at the time you started to tell me about it. Would it be too much to ask for you to give me the background before Pepe comes?"

"What I know, Mister Weaver, it is little. Nobody knows much. Besides my Pepe, one woman in Taos, she saw Miss Ames while she is alive. She is the only one. Mister Nelson he lived there one month only. He stay alone. Nobody know much about him but he paint pictures. A few times I saw him in the store in town, in Seco. That is all."

"Why did he kill her?"

Sanchez shrugged broadly. "Some say he was crazy, some say he kill her for money she bring when she come to him. She come on the bus from Santa Fe the day he kill her."

"From Santa Fe?" Weaver echoed. It gave him a little turn to remember that, since this had happened eight years ago, he'd been in Santa Fe then. He'd spent five years there, up to six years ago when he and Vi had moved to Kansas City.

"Not from Santa Fe she started. They—how do you say?—trail her back to Albuquerque, she stay at hotel there the night before. Before that—?" He shrugged. "Here comes Pepe now, I think."

Weaver hadn't heard anything, but the door opened and Luis came back in, after him a tall, dark and very handsome young Spanish-American. He looked queryingly through the door into the parlor and Sanchez said, "Come in, Pepe. This is Mister Weaver, who has taken the house where Mister Nelson lived. He wants to ask you about what you saw that night. He will write the story about it."

Pepe Sanchez came into the room and Weaver stood and put out his hand; he thought there was a momentary hesitation before Pepe took it.

"What do you want to know?" The young man's voice was faintly sullen.

"Well—just what it was that you saw, Pepe. But, unless you're in a hurry to get back to the dance, may I ask you to come out with me to the place where it happened? That way you can show me just where you were standing and tell me what you saw, right from where you saw it. My car's right outside; it'll take only a few minutes to get there and I'll drive you back, of course." He looked at Sanchez. "And if you'd care to come along, Mr. Sanchez, I'd like to offer you both a drink while we're at my place."

Sanchez smiled and bobbed his head. "Thank you. We will be glad."

He seemed to take Pepe's consent for granted and, after a momentary hesitation, so did Weaver. They went through the crowded room and Sanchez opened the door and held it politely.

Weaver, not to be outdone, went to the wrong side of his coupe and ceremoniously held the door open for Sanchez and Pepe before he went around to the other side and got in under the wheel.

He drove the mile and a half to his house, used the

little bridge to drive onto and back away from so he could park the car facing back toward Arroyo Seco. They got out.

"Now, Pepe," Sanchez said. "Tell to Mister Weaver."

"I was standing here," Pepe said. He'd moved a few steps from the parked car. He pointed. "Through that window I saw into the house. That is the kitchen."

"About what time was this?" Weaver interrupted. He'd have to know the day and the date, too, of course, but he could always find that out from newspapers or court records and he wanted to concentrate now on the eyewitness account he was about to hear.

"About like now. About eight o'clock. I was fishing in the arroyo and was coming home. I was late. I was walking past this house and I was about here—"

"The leg, Pepe," Sanchez prompted.

"I had hurt my ankle, twisted it. That is why I was late. I was limping and could not walk fast. The light was on in the kitchen. I could see through the window—"

"Wait," Weaver said. "I'm sorry to keep on interrupting, but let me go inside and turn on the kitchen light, so it will be just like it was then. That was the only light on?"

"Yes, I think."

Weaver went into the house and turned on the kitchen light. He came out and stood beside Pepe again. "All right," he said.

"Yes, this is where I stood, because I could see the back door like now. The young lady was standing against the door, maybe two steps from it with her back toward it. She was backing slow like she was afraid if she moved fast he would move fast, too, before she could get there. She was very afraid. She had one hand behind her like she was reaching for the doorknob and the other hand was out in front like to hold off the knife."

"And you could see the man, too, Nelson?"

"Yes," Pepe said. "His shoulder, the back of his head. His arm raised with the knife in his hand. It looked like a kitchen knife and he held it wrong, not like you hold a knife for fighting. He held it for stabbing down and that is the wrong way."

"You didn't see his face, then. You're sure it was Nelson?"

"Yes, from the shape of his head I could tell, and from his hair. It was light, like straw, and he wore it very short, straight up."

"A crew cut?"

"I think that's what they call it. And later when he went through the door, the kitchen door, after her I saw some of the side of his face when he turned a little bit. I am sure it was Mr. Nelson."

"But you'd never seen the girl before?"

"No. I did not know there was a woman in the house. Mr. Nelson lived there alone. That was why I first stopped to look when I saw her through the window."

Weaver said, "All right, go on. What happened?"

"She got the door opened and got out before he got to her. And he ran out after her. That was all I saw."

"You didn't see either of them after they went through the door?"

"The house was in between. She ran straight back and it was dark. I heard her scream out once when she was far. That was all. I got home as fast as I could, limping, to tell my father. That is all I know. They did not take me back with them."

Weaver nodded. He wanted to ask the elder Sanchez what had happened after that, but he could ask that while they were inside having the drinks he had suggested. He invited them in and poured three generous glasses from the jug of muscatel. They thanked him as he handed glasses to each of them.

Weaver asked Sanchez, "You came back with the sheriff?"

"Yes. The door was not locked and the lights were not on. He knocked first and called and then he went inside and turned on all the lights. Nothing, he said. We came away."

Weaver sipped his wine and looked at Pepe. "What did Jenny Ames look like?"

"Pretty, I think. Her hair was black but her face was very white. Maybe because she was so afraid. Just a few seconds I saw her. That is all I remember."

"How was she dressed?"

"A green dress, I think."

"Blue, Pepe," Sanchez said. "A blue dress she was found in."

Pepe shrugged. "A blue dress, maybe."

"And can you describe Nelson—outside of his hair? You already told me about that."

"He was tall. Taller than you, and heavier. He was very good-looking, I think. But he was not friendly with people."

"Did anyone see him after that?" Weaver turned to Sanchez again.

"Yes. The sheriff, he did not believe Pepe but he come back next day to talk to Mister Nelson. Mister Nelson said he was driving his car the evening before. He said he never had a woman in his place, that Pepe make mistake. And the sheriff looked around house, inside, outside again by day and he find nothing, nothing to show a woman was there. So the sheriff he left. A day, two days after that Mister Nelson left the house and this country. And two months more is found the body of the woman."

Weaver nodded. There were a lot more questions, but he had his full eyewitness account and he could probably find a better source of other information.

He said, "Uh—Pepe. We took you away from a dance, and I want to get you back. But is there time for another drink?"

"Thank you, Mister Weaver." It was Sanchez who answered, not Pepe. "The dance, it will last late. There is no hurry."

Weaver poured another drink. But he could see from the sullen expression on the boy's face that he didn't enjoy staying, so he set a fast pace in finishing the drink and didn't suggest a third.

He drove them back to Arroyo Seco, dropping Sanchez off at the house and insisting on driving Pepe on to the dance hall, although it was only a few hundred yards further on.

He drove faster going home through the night that suddenly seemed—for no reason he could name—to press about him.

And, when he got there, it seemed to press about the

little adobe house, to press against the panes of the windows once he was inside it.

He poured himself another drink, a stiff one, this time from part of a bottle of whisky that was in the cupboard.

He looked at the kitchen door and shivered a little, almost seeing the girl standing there, terror in her white face under black hair, as she groped behind her for the knob.

Might as well finish the whisky, he decided. He poured himself another but before he started on it he got paper and pencil. He'd better get down notes on Pepe Sanchez's eyewitness story while it was fresh in his mind, while he was sober, and before he might forget any details.

He got it down on paper and the whisky was gone so he poured himself another glass of the wine. It tasted good and he wondered why he'd bothered changing to the whisky first; he'd been acquiring a taste for sweet wine. He'd never really liked the taste of whisky anyway and wine made you just as drunk but with fewer unpleasant aftereffects.

He sat and thought and drank. He looked at his watch and it was a few minutes after eleven and after a long while he looked at his watch again and it was still the same time. So he'd forgotten to wind his watch that morning and now he didn't know what time it was. And he didn't care.

He was drunk and he didn't care about that either. But his bladder did. He went outside and walked to the little bridge along the creek between the house and the road and stood for a minute or two, swaying a bit, at the edge of the bridge. The wind, a cool night wind, blew against him and he wetted his trouser legs very slightly. Who was it had cautioned against pissing against the wind? Oh yes, Rabelais, good old Rabelais. He'd have to get a copy of *Gargantua and Pantagruel* and read it again. Great stuff. The goose's neck and the ring of Hans Carvel and all that.

He was drunk. He looked back at the house, with the kitchen window lighted because he'd been sitting in that room, and then he went on across the bridge and a few steps along the edge of the road.

This was where Pepe Sanchez had stood.

The window, and through it the back door that led out

into the dark night and violent death after a far cry. Beyond a murderer's shoulder and an upraised knife, a frightened, pretty girl with black hair.

Forget it.

Stumble back into the house and sit again at the table. Stare at the door again and picture the girl backed against it. Put yourself into her mind—a madman coming toward her, light glinting from the upraised knife, murder in his face. Pepe had not seen his face, but Jenny had. The door, and night and death beyond.

Funny, Weaver thought, murder really *happens*. He'd never had direct contact with it before; it was just something you read about and you don't disbelieve it but you don't realize it either.

Somehow, he was realizing this one.

He poured himself another drink and then, when he had drunk part of it, the room was going in circling, dizzying swoops that put a feeling in his genitals like the feeling you get in a dropping elevator.

And then it was gray early morning and he lifted his head from the table. There was the sickly smell of vomit somewhere and there was an awful taste in his mouth and yellow fog in his mind.

He wanted water, lots of cold water. Inside him first, then outside. He drank three dippers of it from the bucket he had carried from the stream. He went outside, then, into the cool freshness of the dawn. He stripped off his clothes and walked into the cold shallow stream. He knelt in it and splashed icy water over his body, gasping with the shock of it, but feeling as though he was washing his follies away and that there'd never be another night as foolish as that one.

Cleansed and shivering, he went back into the house. He dried himself off and put on pajamas. He thought, I don't want to wake to *this*, so he cleaned up the vomit and put away the bottle and the jug and the glasses; he made a bundle of the clothes he had stripped off so he could take them in to the cleaner's without having to look at them again. The day was bright by then although the sun was not yet above the mountains; he turned off the light which was still burning a sickly yellow in the bright daylight.

He got under blankets on the bed and he thought: *Why did I do that? I must never do it again.* And then he slept.

When he wakened the position of the sun told him it was almost noon. He got up and dressed, feeling a bit shaky but almost human. There was, while he was dressing, the almost-remembrance of a dream, but he couldn't grasp it; it faded even as his mind reached for it. It didn't matter, he told himself; dreams are random, meaningless things.

He didn't feel up to making coffee for himself so he drove into Taos as soon as he dressed. He had breakfast at the coffee shop at La Fonda and set and wound his watch; it was a quarter of twelve.

He went to the post office and there was no mail for him.

Maybe, he decided, he should go around to the local newspaper—a weekly called *El Crepúsculo*—and get as many of the rest of the facts about the Jenny Ames murder as he could. The sooner he got that off his mind, the better he was going to feel. After last night, he was almost sorry he'd started it. Or would he have got drunk anyway?

It was lunch hour now, just the wrong time to go around. But breakfast had made him feel better and now that he'd eaten, a pickup drink would do him more good than harm, if he held it to one.

He killed time by driving out to Sagebrush Inn, a couple of miles from town in the direction of Santa Fe, for his drink. He held it to two drinks and then it was one-thirty and time for him to try the newspaper office.

The editor, whose desk was just inside the door, was a short, stocky man with sandy hair in a crew cut—like Nelson's, Weaver thought. He introduced himself.

The editor put out a hand. "My name's Callahan, Mr. Weaver. What can I do for you?"

Weaver told him. ". . . so if you've got back files—that is, if your paper goes back eight years—I should have asked that first, I guess."

Callahan grinned. "We go back more than eight years. This is the oldest paper in the Southwest; it was founded in 1835. I'm afraid you'll have to study what you want here, though; we can't let our bound volumes go out."

"That'll be fine," Weaver said.

Callahan left the outer room and came back with a big volume of bound newspapers which he put down on the counter. "This is the year. As I recall it, Jenny Ames' body was found in July—or it could have been August. You'd better start looking in July."

Weaver thanked him and leafed through to the first July issue; there wasn't any headline that sounded likely so he turned on; nothing for the second issue in July. But there was a headline in the third: BODY OF UNIDENTIFIED WOMAN FOUND NEAR SECO.

Callahan had stepped back to the counter beside him. He said, "Yes, I remember now. That story broke on a Wednesday, just before we went to press. You'll find nothing there but the finding of the body. In the next issue you'll get the details—about all of them that were ever known. Would you like paper and pencil?"

"Paper, if I may have some. I have a pencil."

Weaver read the story of the finding of the body. It had been found by one Ramon Camillo, a resident of Arroyo Seco, while out hunting. It had been buried in a very shallow grave in sandy soil, apparently scooped out by hand and hastily covered. A dog or a coyote had dug a hole down to the body, which was under only six or eight inches of dirt, and Camillo had found the grave because of the odor coming from the hole. He had looked down and seen what looked like black human hair and he had moved enough of the sand to be sure that what was buried there really was a human body. He had returned to Seco and had phoned the sheriff in Taos. The sheriff had brought the coroner and a deputy with him and the body had been exhumed. It was considerably decomposed but appeared—according to the coroner, a Dr. Gomez—to be the body of a young woman, dead for about two to two and a half months. The coroner would perform an autopsy and an inquest would be held.

Weaver glanced at Callahan, who was still standing beside him. "Didn't they connect it up, right away, with the story Pepe Sanchez had told them about seeing Nelson chasing a woman with a knife?"

"Freeman—that's the sheriff who was in office then—says he did, but that he was saving that angle until the inquest and until he had a chance to see if he could trace Nelson before the alarm went out. I didn't make the connection myself because I didn't know about the Sanchez boy's story until Freeman told me about it afterwards. At the time we went to press with that first story I didn't even know that it was obvious from first glance that the girl had died of knife wounds—Freeman held that out on me too."

Weaver made a note of the date the body had been found and of the three names that appeared in the story—Ramon Camillo, Sheriff Will Freeman, Dr. Alberto Gomez, the coroner. The rest of it he could remember.

He turned over to the front page of the next week's paper.

The story rated a banner head this time and two and a half columns of the front page. The inquest had been held the previous Tuesday.

Weaver read the story closely and attentively, making notes again of names and dates and relying on his memory for other details. Callahan had gone back to his desk, so there wasn't any hurry. And there ought to be almost enough right here, he thought, to make a story for Luke Ashley. Or maybe not—Luke must have read this too, if he'd spent a few days on the case, and he must have decided something was missing.

The inquest had opened with Ramon Camillo's story of his finding of the body—the same story, with a few added but unimportant details, as had been told in the previous issue.

Then Pepe Sanchez had been put on the stand and had told his story of two months previous. It was substantially the story Pepe had told Weaver the evening before—although it had been more vivid and real there in the dark with Pepe pointing at the lighted window and telling what he had seen from the very spot from which he had seen it.

The sheriff himself had then taken the stand and had told his share of the events of that night. How he'd had the call from Sanchez and had taken a deputy with him to Seco; how they'd gone to Nelson's place but had failed to find anything to substantiate the boy's story and had returned to Taos. How he'd gone out again the next day and had talked to Nelson and had—with Nelson's permission—made an even more thorough investigation and had found nothing suspicious or nothing to contradict Nelson's story that he had never had a woman guest—let alone chased one out into the night with a knife.

Freeman testified that Nelson's reputation had backed up his statement that he had never had a woman guest. Nelson had done occasional moderate drinking at local public places and he had made a few casual acquaintances, but none of them had been women. As far as was known, he had never either visited anyone or been visited. He claimed to be an artist—and had various canvases and painting equipment at his house when the sheriff had searched it—but he had never exhibited locally. Nor, to the knowledge of anyone in Taos, had he ever sold a painting.

The next few witnesses were people who, as the result of slight and casual contacts with Nelson, confirmed—but added little to—what Freeman had already told about Nelson's local reputation and local lack of knowledge concerning him.

The next witness was, next to Pepe, the star of the proceedings; it was she who was able to identify the victim, at least by description and the circumstance of dates, as the girl who, two months before, had ridden up from Santa Fe with her on the bus on the afternoon of the murder—and to supply her name, Jenny Ames.

The witness was Carlotta Evers; she was clerk and bookkeeper at a Taos clothing store.

Miss Evers testified that on the day in question she had been returning from a vacation in Santa Fe and had boarded the afternoon bus for Taos just before it left the bus station at one o'clock. The only seat left vacant was one next to a pretty, dark-haired girl; she had taken that seat and had fallen into conversation, during the several-hour trip, with the girl, who had seemed very eager to talk, especially after she learned that Miss Evers lived in Taos.

She introduced herself as Jenny Ames and said that she was coming to Taos to live, and to marry a man who was then living there. She asked Miss Evers if she knew an artist named Charles Nelson. Miss Evers had not known him.

But she answered innumerable eager questions about Taos itself and the country around it—Jenny Ames had told her that Nelson lived about ten miles out of Taos, past a place called Arroyo Seco—and she said that Jenny Ames had been "starry-eyed" in her eagerness to get there.

The conversation had been casual and two months before and Miss Evers could not remember whether Jenny Ames had mentioned where she came from or not; if even the general section of the country had been mentioned she could not remember it. She did have the impression that it wasn't New Mexico, possibly from the number of questions Jenny Ames had asked about the Spanish-American people who made up the bulk of the population of that state. She couldn't describe Jenny Ames any more accurately than Pepe Sanchez had, except for details of clothing—but the descriptions coincided as far as they went.

Miss Evers testified further that Jenny Ames had told her that her fiancé was meeting her at the bus station in Taos and that she wanted Miss Evers to meet him when they got there. He had written her that he had arranged to reserve a room for her in a hotel in Taos; that he was taking her first to see his own place, where they'd live after they were married, then that he would bring her back to Taos for the night, as the marriage ceremony was arranged for the following day.

Jenny Ames had told her further that she had got to know Charles Nelson through a Lonely Hearts Club that advertised in a magazine, that they had corresponded for a while and then Nelson had come to visit her and had stayed a week in the city—or town—in which she lived, and that during that time they had fallen in love and become engaged, that he couldn't stay there because he was teaching in a Taos art school and was on brief vacation, that he had to return to his job, and that they had subsequently made the arrangement, by correspondence, for her to join him in Taos and marry him there—tomorrow.

When the bus had pulled in, Jenny Ames had introduced Miss Evers to Charles Nelson, who was waiting to greet her. But the couple had seemed—quite understandably—anxious to be alone together and Miss Evers had left them immediately after the introduction. She had already given Jenny Ames her Taos address and had asked her to use it after she was married and settled down. She had seen them get into Nelson's car and drive away.

She was sure of the date because it had been a Sunday, the last day of her vacation, and the dates of her vacation were on record at the clothing store.

Dr. Alberto Gomez, the coroner, had next taken the stand. He testified that he had examined the body and that it was the body of a girl of about twenty—within two years one way or the other—about five feet four inches tall, weighing ( at time of death) probably about a hundred and ten pounds, fair complexion and black hair. It had been buried at least two months. Cause of death had been several knife wounds in the body, almost any one of which could have been fatal. They had been struck with a broad, single-edged knife at least eight inches long. Yes, a kitchen knife— if it was a moderately sharp one—could have been the weapon used.

No, neither Pepe Sanchez nor Carlotta Evers had been called upon to view the body; in its present state of decomposition neither could have been expected to make an identification from having seen the deceased once—and for seconds only, in Pepe's case—two months before. Positive identification would come only from dental records; even fingerprints were unobtainable at this stage. In answer to a question from a member of the jury—yes, the body had been fully clothed and there was no evidence of rape.

Sheriff Freeman was called again to the stand. He testified that he had made a note of the date of his call to Arroyo Seco to investigate the Sanchez boy's story and that it was the same date that Miss Evers had given for her meeting of Jenny Ames and of Charles Nelson, May 17th. He testified that he had checked all hotels, rooming houses and tourist courts in or near Taos and that Charles Nelson had not—as Miss Evers had testified that Jenny Ames had told her—reserved a room for Jenny Ames for that night. Also that no application had been made by Nelson for a marriage license nor had he made arrangements with any local clergyman or civil official to have a marriage performed.

He stated that he had sent out descriptions of Charles Nelson to law-enforcement agencies all over the country and had been attempting to trace his movements after leaving the house beyond Seco, but thus far without success. It had not yet been possible to determine even the exact date of his departure, although it had probably been within a day or two, a few days at the outside, after the murder; he had found no one either in Taos or Seco who had seen Nelson after he, Freeman, had seen him the morning after the murder. Perhaps it had been that interview—although Nelson had come through it without arousing suspicion—that had frightened him into leaving. Until then, Nelson would not have known that the Sanchez boy had seen—what he had seen.

Freeman testified further that he had had no greater success in tracing any of Nelson's movements before he had come to Taos, about six weeks before the murder. He had paid his rent for the house beyond Seco in cash and in advance and had given no references. If he had ever mentioned anything concerning his past to anyone in Taos, that person had not yet come forward—and the sheriff wished that he would.

Nor had Freeman been able to find where Jenny Ames had come from or any facts about her except what she had told Carlotta Evers. Inquiries were still being made—and the nation-wide publicity being given the case should bring reports from somewhere, soon.

The coroner's jury had been out twelve minutes and had brought in a verdict of willful murder.

Weaver made his final notation and then turned to the front page of the following issue. The only story was a statement by the sheriff that the inquiry into the murder of Jenny Ames was being continued and that a lead to the whereabouts of Charles Nelson had been obtained.

In the next issue there was nothing.

He left the volume open on the counter and turned around to Callahan's desk, waited till the editor looked up.

"Anything further after that one issue?"

"Not a thing, Mr. Weaver. The story died on its feet after the inquest. They never did find out where Jenny Ames came from nor where Nelson came from or went to."

"What was the lead on Nelson the sheriff thought he had the following week?"

"Damn if I even remember. Whatever it was, it petered out."

Weaver closed the bound volume and stood looking at it a moment. He stood there long enough to light a cigarette and then turned back to the editor's desk.

"Thanks a lot," he said. "I'd like to buy you a drink; can you knock off long enough?"

Callahan glanced at his watch. "Shouldn't. But I will." They went around the corner to El Patio and found a table and ordered drinks. Callahan turned to watch the Spanish-American girl who had taken their order go back indoors toward the bar. "Jail-bait," he said. "When those Spanish gals look eighteen, they're probably fourteen." He sighed. "Well, it's fun to window-shop. Say, I hear someone has taken the place Nelson lived in. Is it you? Is that part of your interest in the case?"

"I'm the one who took it. But I wouldn't be interested just for that reason; I told you the truth about why I'm looking it up. By the way, didn't the girl have any luggage?"

"Yes, she got off the bus with two suitcases and Nelson put them in his car. But they weren't found; he must have taken them with him when he left."

Weaver frowned. "A funny case. Especially in that they never traced the girl back farther than they did. Of course it was a pretty cold trail by that time, but even so—"

He broke off as their drinks came. Callahan's eyes followed the girl back to the door again, and then he turned back. "That part of it was strange, all right. The case got fairly wide publicity and you'd think someone who knew the girl would have read about the murder—or that she'd have been reported missing wherever she came from." The editor shrugged. "But she may have come from some one-horse town where nobody happened to read about it. That's what most of us figured."

Weaver suggested, "Or possibly the woman who talked to her on the bus got the name wrong. I mean, it might have been Jenny Haines or Jenny James or something like that."

"No, it was Ames all right. She signed it—Oh, that's one thing that did come up later, after what you read. They did trace her as far as Albuquerque; she stayed at a hotel there the night before the murder. She registered there as Jenny Ames."

"They never found the Lonely Hearts agency through which Nelson got into correspondence with her?"

Callahan shook his head. "That angle was tried—and Uncle Sammy's boys did the asking because the U. S. mails would have been involved. But no dice; those outfits don't keep records of individual correspondents, once they've turned them over to other correspondents and collected their fee. I suppose they'd have to have warehouses full of files if they did. Well, I'm afraid I'd better push back to the office—still have some work to do for today."

"Sure you won't have another drink?"

"I'll take a rain check. Thanks." Callahan pushed back his chair and stood.

Weaver said, "Wait a minute. I just had a thought that's so ridiculously simple someone else *must* have had it eight years ago, but I don't see the catch in it. You say she signed the register in an Albuquerque hotel. There's always a blank where you put down where you came from; didn't Jenny Ames fill it out?"

"She filled it out, but she put down 'Taos, N. M.' She planned to marry here and stay here so she must have figured this was her real address." Callahan smiled grimly. "Well—she stayed here all right."

**N**ight again, pressing against the windowpanes. Silence except for the far wild yapping of the coyotes.

And Weaver, sober tonight—although he was sipping a little wine as he tried to read—found the night and the silence, for the first time, just a bit frightening.

You see, other evenings here he'd been alone. Tonight—not quite. Jenny Ames was there, somehow. Today, when he had learned the little about her that there was to be known, she'd come alive for him. Yesterday she'd been a name.

Tonight her presence was in the room, in his mind. She was the more vivid to him because he knew so little about her. A photograph, had one existed, would have spoiled the illusion—but there was no photograph, only vague description with which his imagination could do as it willed. A pretty girl, young, with black hair, who had loved—or thought she loved—a monster and who had come to marry him.

Out of mystery she had come. And into deeper mystery, the ultimate mystery, she had gone. And she had been in this very room, perhaps sat in this very chair, during the few hours that had elapsed between her arrival here and her leaving—into the final darkness.

Never to return. Never to answer the questions left behind her.

*Where did you come from, Jenny? Why did no one trace you here? Did no one love you, care about you, in the place from which you came? What had life and people done to you, Jenny, that had made you so desperate as to write to a Lonely Hearts Club, to meet and love a murderer?*

*What made you love him, Jenny? What wiles did he use on you, that time he visited the town you lived in? How did he make you love him so?*

*So many questions left behind you.*

*Why did he kill you, Jenny? Because he was mad and for that reason only? Or was there gain for him somehow, and method in his madness? And did you know, before you died, why you died?*

*Did you have time to think, in those awful minutes after you saw the knife and before you felt it, time to wonder, time to realize that he had planned it all?*

*And he had planned it, Jenny. No room had been taken for you, no arrangements for a wedding made. He brought you here to kill you. But why?*

Those damned coyotes, he thought. No, they weren't new to him. In the years he'd lived in Santa Fe he'd heard them often—never, of course, from his quarters in town, but whenever he'd driven out of town and into wild country. Often at night he'd stopped his car along a road and shut off the engine and the lights to sit there listening, enjoying—or was it enjoying?—the wild loneliness of that sound, the primitive unanswerable yearning in it.

Tonight it was getting on his nerves.

*Did you ever hear that sound, Jenny? Possibly not, for it was soon after darkness fell that you died, and perhaps they had not yet started their nightly lament against the wailing wall of the sky. Or had they started, back there in the hills? Did you run toward that sound as toward a lesser evil?*

He poured himself more wine and thought *nuts;* he'd be going crazy himself if he let himself keep thinking like that. He'd found out, now, all there was to be found out about Jenny Ames and he'd better write it up from his notes and send it to Luke so it would be off his mind. Should he rent a typewriter in Taos tomorrow instead of waiting till Vi came with his portable?

But something told him he wouldn't get it off his mind that easily.

Was it just because he lived here where it had happened? Well, that was part of it, but it was more than that. This interest in Jenny Ames—was it because, when he'd started this, he'd been interested in nothing and therefore what might have otherwise been a normal interest had become a compelling one? Yes, that could be it.

But it was more than that.

Why? Was it something within himself? An aftermath of his breakdown, his—face it—his teetering on the brink of ·madness those weeks in the san, that now was going to give him an obsession with an eight-year-old crime, a girl eight years dead? Was his interest psychopathic, abnormal?

Or was it, after all, just a normal interest, accentuated a bit perhaps by his lack of interest in other things? Wasn't the mystery of the crime—and of its victim and its motive—sufficient to interest anyone? The fact that Jenny hadn't been traced, that almost nothing was known about her, where she had come from and what she had been—why hadn't those simple things come to light?

Nelson—that was different; it's understandable why a killer's past and his movements after he has successfully committed a crime are going to be hard to learn. Especially the latter, when he has a two months' start before the fact that he has killed is known. And if, as seemed probable, he had planned to kill even before he came here, obviously the name he gave was false and he would have said nothing, left no clue, through which his true identity and his antecedents could be learned.

But Jenny.

*Did you have a secret, Jenny?*

He swore at himself and tried to stop thinking about it.

He tried again to read and he couldn't concentrate on the book at all. And it was only nine o'clock; he couldn't possibly go to sleep after having slept so late that morning.

He'd *have* to get himself something to do or try to do evenings besides reading. God, even a deck of cards to play solitaire. Or maybe he should try to write; he'd wanted to write a novel once, but that had been a long time ago and the vague idea he'd had seemed silly now. God, no wonder; that had been in his late teens, twenty years ago.

No, he'd never write that novel now, or any other. But shorter things, perhaps? He wished again that he'd brought his typewriter. Maybe factual things would be easy to write. He wondered if a job like Luke's—digging up facts on past or recent crimes—would be interesting. Well, he was having a chance to find out if he could do writing like that, if he wanted to try his hand at it. Maybe he should write the article about Jenny Ames himself. Not try to sell it himself, of course; that wouldn't be fair to Luke because the whole thing had been Luke's idea. But possibly instead of sending Luke merely notes to work from he should surprise him by sending him the story ready written. His style and approach might be way off the beam—at least unless he studied some fact detective magazines first to familiarize himself with them—but that wouldn't matter; Luke could rewrite it. But even if Luke submitted it as originally written, he'd rather have Luke use his own by-line and they could split even on the deal, because it would be Luke's by-line that would sell the story and make it get Luke's rates instead of beginner's rates. Or should he—? No, real estate was his racket, not writing. This one story and never tackle another.

He tried to read again and found, after a while, that again he'd been reading the same paragraph over and over and still didn't know what it said.

He put down the book and took another sip of wine. It was sweet wine and he'd found it particularly good for solitary drinking such as this. He could go through all the motions of drinking and feel the effect, eventually even get a bit drunk, but not with the devastating completeness of whisky. And *never* whisky and wine both; that's what had got him last night. Wine alone made him merely mellow and fuzzy around the edges, and it was sometimes nice to be fuzzy around the edges.

But, whisky or wine, he had been drinking a lot since he'd come here.

All right, damn it, he thought; you've been bored stiff most of the time and you might as well admit it. The mountains are God damn beautiful but you can't look at mountains all the time; the air is wonderful, but breathing isn't enough. And you can't read and you can't paint and—

He was staring at the door and tried, suddenly, to wrench his mind away from the thing it was trying to picture there.

And then he thought, *why? Why should I?*

*So the doctor told you to get interested in something, and you've found something that interests you and you keep fighting to keep your mind away from it. Anything except making money, the doctor said, and this makes money only slightly and incidentally; you've already got enough data to send Luke, if that's as far as your interest went.*

*So maybe your interest verges on the psychopathic, but if you don't get interested in something, you'll go crazy anyway, so—*

He felt better, lots better.

He looked at the kitchen door and *let* himself think. He remembered the angle of vision he'd had from the outside, when he'd stood where Pepe Sanchez had stood, and tried to visualize and place the figures as they'd stood when Pepe had first seen them. Let's see—the table had been moved—but when he'd first seen the place it had been about three feet farther from the door. He moved it back and—yes, that was better. Nelson would have been standing beside the table when Pepe first saw him, probably just having taken the knife from its drawer. And Jenny *there*, in line between the window and the back door, moving backwards toward the door.

Weaver went to the back door and opened it, staring out into the moonless dark. For the moment, the coyotes were silent; the whole night was completely silent, utterly without sound.

From somewhere back there in the distant dark his mind seemed to hear the eight-year-old echo of a far cry, the one scream Jenny Ames had screamed. Had it been when she first knew that the killer was going to catch her?

Had there been a moon that night? Stars? He hadn't thought to ask Pepe, he hadn't thought that it mattered, and it hadn't then. But it mattered now; it mattered because he was interested, because he wanted to know what that night had been like, just as he wanted to know what Jenny had been like—and even Nelson.

There was no moon tonight, just a faint glimmer of starlight. But he could see easily now that his eyes had accustomed themselves to the lack of light. He could make out the outline of the outhouse and, beyond it, the shed. And beyond them the ground was level, sandy, sloping slightly upward toward the foothills of the mountains.

He walked out, leaving the kitchen door open behind him—as it would have been left open that night long ago—and found that he could see the clumps of chamiso, the line of cottonwoods in the distance to the left, pale white like skeletons in the starlight.

A girl, running.

He stood there for what seemed like a very long time. Then there was the sound of a car coming along the road toward the house, from Seco. Unless someone was lost—on a road that petered out to nothing less than half a mile beyond this house, the last one—then the car was coming here.

He walked around the outside of the house in time to see the oncoming headlights slow down and stop directly in front.

"Hi, Weaver. Up and about? Want to talk awhile?"

It was Callahan's voice. Weaver called, "Sure, come on in," and the lights of the car went off. Callahan got out and walked across the bridge from the car. "Bit late for a call," he said, "but I thought I'd see if your lights were on."

"It isn't late," Weaver said. He glanced at his wrist watch and saw that it was only half-past nine; he'd thought it was considerably later than that. "Glad to have some company for a change."

He wondered if he was lying about that; he *was* glad to see Callahan, but maybe it was because he could pump him, now that he was here, for more details about Jenny Ames. Several questions had occurred to him that the editor might be able to answer.

Inside, Callahan said, "Got it fixed up pretty good. Did I tell you that I live on this road too? Third house back, about a quarter of a mile. Out in this country that makes me one your neighbors."

"Glad you live so near," Weaver told him. "Let's go in the kitchen—that's my sitting room. And can I offer you some muscatel? Sorry, but it's all I've got on hand."

"Well—one. My wife's in Santa Fe, went down there for a duplicate bridge tournament and she's staying overnight with friends. I got a little restless and thought I'd drive down this way and see if your lights were on. If they hadn't been, I'd have gone back; it's a little late for a call."

"Don't sound so damn formal," Weaver said. "So drop in at three in the morning if you feel like it and my lights are on." He poured wine into a glass and handed it to Callahan, then refilled his own glass. "What time do people go to bed around here anyway?"

"The Spanish people—and that's most of them out this way—about nine o'clock. They think we Anglos are crazy—and maybe they're right."

"Maybe they are at that," Weaver said. "Which reminds me. Do they like us?"

"Well—no. Not particularly."

"I thought so. I'm not new to Spanish-Americans, not after living five years in Santa Fe. I even know enough to call them that and not Mexicans. But I've noticed a difference in Arroyo Seco. They're polite as hell, but—"

"*Salud,*" Callahan said. "They're polite as hell but— That's just about it."

There was a sloppiness to Callahan's enunciation that made Weaver look at him more closely and he saw now that the editor was already a bit drunk; his face was slightly flushed and his eyes were beginning to be glassy. Obviously he'd been drinking before he came here, possibly alone at home.

Weaver said, "But why? I mean, why more than in Santa Fe or other towns where Spanish-Americans and Anglos live together? Why especially in Taos?"

"Oh, not Taos. Just Arroyo Seco—this is one of the last strongholds of the old-line Spanish-Americans that hate Anglo ways and everything about Anglos. Especially ones like us who try to live out here among them—taking over their land, buying it when they have to sell—and then fixing it so they can never get it back."

"How do you mean, fixing it so they can't get it back?"

"Fixing it up too well. Take this place, just for an example. The people who lived here before Nelson did bought it for five hundred dollars—the Spanish-American family who lived here, at least a dozen of them, had a bad year and deaths in the family and doctor bills. It was a two-room place then, falling apart. So five hundred was a fair price. But what do the Robinsons—that was their name—do? They fix it up. They add a room; they fix the floors and the woodwork; they put in two oil burners instead of one wood stove. They have electricity run from the last house a quarter-mile back. They put up a new outhouse and add a shed. So—now the property's worth a couple of thousand instead of five hundred and none of the natives out here can ever buy it back; it's fancy, it's only for *ricos*, rich people. The average cash income for those people is only a couple of hundred dollars a year. A place like this is a palace to most of them."

"Well, *I* didn't fix it up. I see what you mean, though. I felt it in Seco, when I stopped at the tavern one night."

"I don't. Stop there, I mean. I speak enough Spanish to catch phrases I'm not supposed—or am I?—to overhear. But even if you didn't speak Spanish you could feel the antagonism. Not that I blame them; we're changing this country, their way of life. We're interlopers. They've lived here practically since Coronado. But don't let it worry you, Weaver."

"Worry me how?"

"I mean they're not going to come here some night to assassinate you or anything like that. Just don't tangle with them, outside of business. Let them alone and they'll let you alone. But do your drinking in Taos and you'll like it better. Just be polite to them as they are to you, but don't think you can make friends. There's a barrrier."

Callahan took another sip of his wine. "And it's probably good for us. Gives us the wrong side of race prejudice. We damn Anglos are prejudiced against any minority group we live with; does us good to *be* a minority group and get the dirty end of the stick for once. Sure, the reasons aren't completely logical or justified—but are the reasons we're prejudiced against Jews or Negroes or Chinamen any better? It's good for our immortal souls, if any, to be hated a bit. Do you realize, Weaver, that almost every other country in the world—even those that are on 'our side'—hates us more or less because of what we are? So let's have a sample of it right here at home; maybe it'll teach us we're not completely God's chosen people."

"Ummm," Weaver said. "Maybe you've got something there."

"Yeah, good for us. You know, I had something I wanted to tell you, but damned if I can remember what it was."

"Something about Jenny Ames?"

"I think it was, but I can't remember it right now. Well, I'll think of it some other time. How are you and Jenny getting along?"

Weaver felt himself bristle a little, and then wondered why he had.

"Got about all I need," he said. "I've got Pepe Sanchez's eyewitness account and the newspaper story. That's really enough, but I'd still like to talk to a few people who remember it, if they're still around. Who is?"

"Well, Freeman's not still around; he died a couple of years ago. Doc Gomez, who was coroner then, is still alive, but he's living up in Colorado somewhere. Alamosa, I think. Let's see—who else was there?"

"The woman who rode up on the bus with her. Evers?"

"Sure, Carlotta Evers. She's still in Taos. Works at the supermarket on the west side of the plaza. But be careful—or are you married?"

"I'm married," Weaver said. "Who else might be around? Let's see—there was the man who found the body. Ramon Camillo, I think his name was."

"I don't know. He was from Seco, maybe he still lives there. I didn't know him, aside from seeing him at the inquest."

"The people who knew Nelson, who'd talked to him. Who were they?"

"Don't know, offhand. I guess I knew him as well as any-body else, which means I'd talked to him three or four times. Once his car broke down in front of my place and he couldn't get it started. I wandered out to see if I could help and he said sure if I had a phone he'd like to use it to have a repairman come out from Taos. So I phoned the A-1 and they sent out a man and got his car going. I forget what was wrong with it, but it wasn't anything serious; the mechanic had it running ten minutes after he got there."

"Did Nelson wait inside your place?"

"Sure, when I insisted. I gave him a drink, even, but he wouldn't take a second one. Which reminds me, I will, if I may."

Weaver poured it.

"Didn't Nelson tell you anything at all about himself?"

"Sure. A pack of lies. I remembered most of it when they were looking for him but when it got checked back on, none of it was true. Said he'd come here from a little town in California, Gersonville. Turned out there isn't any town in California by that name. That he'd lived in Woodstock, New York—that's another artists' colony like Taos is—but they couldn't find anyone in Woodstock that knew him, ei-ther by name or description. But he really was an artist, or tried to be one. I'm no judge, but Will Freeman says the place out here was littered with canvases."

"What happened to them? Did he take them all along with him?"

"Guess so, I don't know. I never heard anything to the contrary."

Weaver looked at him thoughtfully. "You say you're no judge. That sounds as though you'd seen some of his paintings. Did you?"

"Some of his water colors, that time his car broke down. He'd been out painting somewhere and was on his way back and while we were talking he showed me what he'd just done. I was polite about it, sure, but it made nuts to me. It was supposed to be mountains, but *what* mountains I couldn't guess—and I've seen all the scenery for lots of miles around here. Oh sure, I know there's such a thing as abstract art and that some of it is supposed to be good, but if this was—well, as I said, I'm no judge."

"You never saw any of his oil paintings?"

"No, and the only person I know of who did see them was Freeman—the two times he was in Nelson's place looking around, the night of the murder and the day after. He wasn't any judge of painting either, but he said they looked like crap to him. As I told you, I think, Nelson never had any guests out here. The only two people known to have been inside the place while he lived here were Jenny Ames and the sheriff. Those water colors, though, they looked to me like something an insane man might do."

"About that day he was inside your place talking to you," Weaver said. "You say what he told you was malarkey, but what—well, what impression did he make on you? What did he seem to be?"

"Well, I think he was queer. And I don't mean strange, I mean homosexual. My guess is that Jenny Ames was pretty safe with him those few hours after she got there and before he killed her. And I'm not alone, incidentally, in thinking Nelson was probably queer—that's the impression he gave other people around Taos—and Taos is pretty good at judging. It gets a lot of them. I guess any artists' colony does. Lezzies, too."

Callahan sipped his wine. "Freeman had the same idea, that Nelson was as queer as a bedbug. One reason why he doubted Pepe's story—he didn't see what Nelson would be doing with a girl out there to begin with."

Weaver was interested. "You're fairly sure of that? I mean that he was straight homo—not even ambivalent?"

"Ninety-nine percent sure, and I'm pretty good at guessing. For instance, *you're* not homo."

"Thanks," Weaver said. "But let's stick to Nelson. Anything else about him you can remember?"

"Well, I wouldn't be surprised if he was a lunger. T. b. He looked big and husky, but that's the kind that often gets it. And he had one coughing spell in my house that sounded like it to me—and I noticed that he coughed carefully into his handkerchief. Besides, he had slight flushed spots in his cheeks—unless they were make-up, and he wasn't *that* queer; he didn't swish. You know it's a funny thing about homos—the masculine-looking kind, not the out-and-out pansies—how girls will fall for them. And fall hard. Girls who haven't been around enough, that is, to spot them as competition instead of prospects. And most of them can be charming as hell when they want to turn on the charm. Nelson didn't, around here, but he probably could have. And he was handsome enough to make women fall for him."

"You're doing fine," Weaver said. "Any other impressions about him?"

"Not that I can remember. Damn, what was it I was going to tell you? With that pumping you've been doing, I've been telling you everything else but. Well, it couldn't have been too important or I'd have remembered it. If I think of it in time I'll let you know. Guess I'd better push along."

"Why? It's still early, not much after ten."

"Sure, but tomorrow's Wednesday, our big day. The day before we go to press. I'll have to get down early—and bright. Thanks for the drinks."

Weaver walked with Callahan to the car and stood on the bridge until the car went out of sight along the curving road. He decided that he rather liked Callahan—and certainly Callahan had been helpful in filling out his picture of Nelson. But—didn't that picture make the motive of the crime even more murky than it had been?

Or did it? A homosexual perhaps fighting his homosexuality, trying to make himself respond to a woman who loved him, suddenly going berserk with hatred and revulsion when he couldn't?

It seemed possible. Only, of course, if Nelson had been psychopathic—aside from or in addition to his homosexuality—to begin with.

But the tuberculosis—if Callahan was right about it—where did it fit into the picture? Perhaps it didn't; perhaps it was incidental.

Weaver turned around and found himself staring into the window of the still lighted kitchen. And again trying to picture what Pepe Sanchez had seen there.

He shook himself a little.

Nuts, he told himself, I'm letting this get me.

Back in the foothills the coyotes were yapping again, their nightly chorus of the damned yearning for the unattainable.

Weaver leaned against the wall and stared up at the stars. A long distance away he could still hear the faint sound of Callahan's car.

The stars, the silly, far, twinkling stars. Somewhere he'd read that the nearest one was eight light-years away. That meant that the light he was seeing from it now, tonight, had left it eight years ago, perhaps on the very night— He shook himself a little. It was all right to let himself get interested in—this—but he couldn't let it *get* him like that.

He went back into the house and decided that for once he was going to bed early and reasonably sober. He did.

**H**e woke, the next morning, in time to see the sun come up over the mountains. It was beautiful; the cool morning air was good to breathe. Life was suddenly good, until he remembered the date.

It was Wednesday, the 31st of May. Tomorrow was the first day of June, the day the girls would go to camp, and Vi would be coming. Strange that she hadn't written already, telling him when to meet her in Santa Fe.

Well, if she didn't write in time, that was her grief and she could take the bus, much as she hated riding buses. Not that he blamed her for that—although there were plenty of things he did blame her for. Indirectly, he knew damned well, the animosity between them (which they kept so carefully submerged for the sake of the girls) had been the cause of the breakdown he'd had. The direct reason, of course, had been that he'd worked too hard, far too hard. But if he analyzed the reasons *why* he'd worked too hard, there were two of them, simple and obvious. First, in order to spend less time in an intolerable home. Second, in order to try (vainly) to earn enough money so he could provide separate maintenance for them, enable them to live apart without the necessity of a divorce—and all the things that a divorce would do to girls the ages of Ellen and Betty.

But the money part hadn't worked out; instead he'd toiled himself into a breakdown that had set him back to scratch again, now with no possibility of a separation in the foreseeable future. Not even the possibility of their living apart this summer while he was recovering.

Another part of it had been his own fault, the drinking. Drinking too much makes any problem worse.

And Vi drank too much, too. That really put the lid on it.

He made coffee for himself and fried two eggs, and then managed to kill a little time washing the few dishes and glasses that were dirty and straightening up and dusting the house.

If he had his typewriter—

The hell with a typewriter; he'd better make at least some notes in longhand before he forgot some of the things he'd learned. All he had on paper were names and dates and all the other details—especially things like those Callahan had told him last night—were still in his head.

He found writing paper and worked for about an hour. When he'd finished, it was still only nine o'clock, far too early to go into Taos for mail. He felt a little better now than he had a few days ago when he'd tried painting last; maybe he should try it again now.

But that reminded him of something else. All those canvases of Nelson's that the sheriff had seen around the house when he'd called here after the murder. Was it possible that some of them, or even some sketches, had been left behind? Possibly somewhere inside the house where he hadn't looked, possibly in the wooden shed twenty yards behind the house? He'd looked in that shed just once to date; he'd decided that he wouldn't need it for anything so he'd merely glanced in and noticed that it seemed to contain only junk, some odds and ends of broken furniture, some rusty bedsprings, an empty oil drum. He'd scarcely stepped inside and hadn't bothered to inventory the contents. There might be some pictures there.

There were. He went through the house systematically first and didn't find so much as a pencil sketch, but in the shed were three unframed canvases tilted with their faces against the wall. They were very dirty, but the shed had been dry and they were intact. He took them out into the sunlight and then got a rag from the house to wipe them off. He put them in a neat row, face out this time, against the side of the shed and stepped back to study them.

They weren't bad.

They were considerably better, anyway, than anything he himself could ever hope to do. They weren't really *good*, however; he knew enough about art to feel sure of that. But there was deep sincerity in them; the man who'd painted them had considered himself to be a serious artist and had done his best.

They were all pictures of mountains, but they were mountains in such shapes and colors as mountains have never been. They were mountains that writhed in dark agony against spectral skies. They were mountains of another dimension, on another world under an alien sun.

Weaver said "Jesus Christ" softly, and not irreverently, to himself as he studied then.

The pictures weren't signed, but they didn't have to be. He knew that they were Nelson's—and he knew that they meant two things; that Nelson was a little mad and that he had had at least a touch of genius to have expressed that madness so perfectly in paint on canvas.

He took them inside the house and propped them up on the table, one after another, to study them in light that was not so glaring.

He'd lost all inclination to get out his own water colors.

He drove in to Taos and it was ten-thirty, still far too early

to find mail at the post office. He drove past Doughbelly
Price's office and saw through the window that Price was
seated at his desk, still wearing the big hat. Weaver parked
his Chevvie and went in. Doughbelly looked up. "Hi,
Weaver. You and the house getting along all right together
out there?"

"We're doing fine," Weaver said. "Listen, out in the shed
behind the house I found three paintings. Not signed but I
think they're by Nelson. Who owns them?"

"I guess I do. Nelson hadn't paid his second month's rent
yet and so I was told that any stuff he left behind him was
mine, which wasn't much. But I didn't notice no paintings.
Where were they?"

"In the shed, against the wall."

"Hell, I remember now, I did see them when I looked
through the joint after Nelson had high-tailed. I looked at
'em, and they looked to me like the rest of the junk in the
shed. Why? They ain't worth anything. Sit down."

Weaver sat down. "I rather like them," he said. "Whether
they're worth anything or not I don't know, but I'd like to
have them."

Doughbelly Price's eyes twinkled under the brim of the
Stetson. "You're going to be gypped if you offer me anything for them. I asked a friend of mine, ran a gallery here
then, whether Nelson's stuff had any commercial value. He
said no. Said Nelson had wanted to exhibit there and had
shown him a few things and they weren't worth nothing."

"That's good," Weaver said, "because I couldn't offer you
much anyway."

"Tell you what, Weaver, how's this for a deal? It wouldn't
hurt the value of the place out there none to have a few pictures hanged on the walls, no matter how lousy the pictures are. So how about this? You get all three of the things
framed—there's lots of places around here does framing—
and hang 'em. When you leave here take one of 'em, to
cover getting the three framed—any one you want—and
leave the other two. Or if you still want all three, we'll
dicker then."

"Done," Weaver said.

He left his car parked where it was and walked to and

around the plaza, looking into windows, killing time until he could get his mail. There'd surely be a letter from Vi today telling him when to meet her.

Somebody said, "Hi, Weaver," and he turned. It was Callahan.

Weaver said, "Hi. How'd you go for a drink?" He'd figured it was too early to have a drink alone, but having one with someone would take the curse off it.

The editor shook his head regretfully. "My busy day, remember? Just ducked out for a cup of coffee. Can I buy you one?"

Weaver decided he might as well have a cup of coffee. At least it would kill time. They went to the coffee shop at La Fonda and sat at the counter.

Callahan shoveled two teaspoons of sugar into his. "Guess I was a little tight when I drove over to your place last night. Sorry I barged in on you so late."

"Don't be foolish. You got there early and left early, and it did me good to have someone to talk to. I've been spending too much time alone since I've been here."

"Your wife's coming soon?"

"Yes."

"Be glad to meet her. Say, I remembered, as soon as I got home, what it was I'd been wanting to tell you about the Nelson business. I remembered about the one report they got on him after he left here. Amarillo.

"In the Texas Panhandle?"

"Yes. When they circulated reports on him after the body had been found, a report came in from there. Two months before—a day or two after he left Taos, it must have been— he stayed one night at an Amarillo hotel."

"Under what name?"

"His own. I mean, Charles Nelson. And he registered from Taos. He must have felt sure there was no pursuit after him yet, that the body hadn't been found."

Weaver said, "He must have been heading east then. Anyone there remember anything about him?"

"Not worth mentioning. The name clicked with the hotel clerk when he read about the murder here in Taos and he checked back on the register and found it. But he remembered Nelson himself only well enough to verify the description. He told the police there and they checked around and found the garage where he'd left his car overnight—piled high with luggage and canvases and stuff. And the attendant there thought he remembered—he wasn't too sure—that Nelson had asked about the roads down to El Paso."

"El Paso? Hell, if he was going to El Paso, he'd not have gone by way of Amarillo from Taos. That's two legs of a triangle—it'd be at least a couple hundred miles out of his way."

"More than that, I think. It could have been that he had business in Amarillo, of course. But, more likely, he was heading on east and asked about roads to the south just to throw off anybody that might be trying to trace him later."

"But why, in that case, register under the name they'd be looking for him under?"

"Easy answer to that. He cashed some traveler's checks. Had three twenty-dollar checks left in a book of them, in the name of Nelson, and cashed them at the hotel he stayed at. He must not have figured it was much of a risk, but he might have taken the extra precaution—it didn't cost anything—to ask about roads in the wrong direction, just in case."

Weaver said, "About the traveler's checks. Couldn't they—?"

"They did," Callahan interrupted. "Sure, they traced the ones he'd cashed there, and found they'd been bought in Denver three months before; he'd bought a book of ten of them at a bank there. The other seven turned out to have been cashed in Taos during the time he was living here. He must have realized, after he lammed out, that he still had three uncashed twenty-dollar traveler's checks and took the slight chance of registering under his own name—if Nelson *was* his own name—one night so he could get his sixty bucks out of them. It was a minor and calculated risk; the chance was remote that the body would have been found so soon—if, in fact, it ever was found. Way back there in the hills, he probably figured it was safe forever."

"Did they do any checking in Denver, where he bought the traveler's checks?"

"Oh, sure, but he must have been just passing through. He bought them for cash at a bank where he was a stranger and no other lead to him turned up there at all. Well, I'd better get back to the office."

Callahan insisted on paying the check for the coffees and Weaver let him; the amount wasn't enough to argue about.

They went out to the plaza and started around it; at the corner Weaver pointed. "Is that the supermarket Carlotta Evers works at?"

"Yes. Want to meet her?"

"I'd like to, if you're not in too much of a hurry—"

"Not so much I can't spare another two minutes. Come on."

Business wasn't rushing, at that hour, in the supermarket. Callahan led Weaver to one of the cash-out registers where a dark-haired woman of about thirty or thirty-five—she looked as though she might be half Spanish, half Anglo—quite pretty, was ringing up an order of groceries. There was no one in line behind the customer and as soon as he'd carried his bag of groceries away, Callahan introduced Weaver and explained his interest in Jenny Ames.

Weaver said, "I'd like to talk to you about it, Miss Evers. May I take you to dinner tonight?"

Her smile showed a gold tooth that made her look slightly less attractive. "Thanks. I'd be glad to."

"Where and when shall I meet you?"

"Well—would six be too early? I get off at five and that would give me time to dress. I live right near here, just past the Harwood."

Weaver said that six would he fine and absorbed complicated directions—all directions in Taos are complicated—about how to find the right door.

Another customer approached the register then, and Weaver took his leave and walked back to the newspaper office with Callahan. From there to the post office; it was time now for the first mail to be in.

There was a letter from Vi:

"Dear Georgie—"

His skin crawled a bit at the grammar, spelling and punctuation that followed ( no matter how ridiculous he knew it was that he should feel that way), but its purport was simple. She would take the girls to camp Friday; she herself would leave Kansas City late Saturday afternoon; her train would reach Santa Fe at six o'clock Sunday morning. She was glad that he was going to meet her. The girls sent their love.

He wondered irritably why she couldn't have chosen a train that arrived at a reasonable hour; there were several every day and there was no reason why she had to choose one that got in at such an ungodly time. He'd have to get up at about three o'clock in the morning to meet that train; either that or drive to Santa Fe on Saturday and stay at a hotel there. Probably that would be the lesser of the evils.

Besides, the information was incomplete; the train didn't get into Santa Fe at six o'clock or any other time. The nearest passenger stop for Santa Fe is Lamy, eighteen miles away, and the trains connect there with a bus that carries passengers the final lap into Santa Fe. From her letter he couldn't tell whether the train got into Lamy at six o'clock or whether that was the time the connecting bus reached Santa Fe.

He'd been intending to drive to Lamy to meet the train itself, but since she was so inconsiderate about the time of her arrival, let her take the bus, he decided, into Santa Fe and he'd meet her there. He bought an airmail postcard at the window and wrote and addressed it at the post office desk; he told her to buy her ticket through to Santa Fe, which would make it include the eighteen-mile bus trip from Lamy, and that he'd meet her at the terminal in Santa Fe. He postscripted a reminder about the typewriter and the camera.

That about filled the postcard, but he remembered something else and bought another one; he told Vi that if she'd either bring or ship ahead of her a few blankets and a few assorted dishes, silverware and cooking utensils, it would save them from having to buy more to supplement the few he had already bought, and would save them some money. He was getting a bit worried about money.

Partly on account of money he decided against having lunch in Taos and drove back to the house to cook something for himself; he'd be feeding Carlotta Evers at a restaurant tonight and that would be enough eating expense for one day.

He cooked himself some ham and eggs. It wasn't too good, but it wasn't too bad either—at least as good as Vi could have cooked it; she was incorrigibly careless in her cooking and sloppy in her housework. Neither praise nor censure could induce her to take the little extra trouble that made the difference between a good meal and a poor one. And she had an aversion to trying any new dishes; she cooked the same things over and over again in the same mediocre way—

Well, he had plenty of faults of his own, he thought; and food was not too important a part of his life. Neither, for that matter, was sex, these last few years; he'd done without it most of the time and could keep on doing without it. But if Vi could only talk intelligently, or even listen intelligently, if only she'd read something besides trashy love story and confession magazines—if she could only be a companion, even in the slightest degree—

Don't be an ass, he told himself; that isn't Vi's fault. It's yours.

It was his own fault for having married suddenly and on the basis of a purely physical attraction—and nothing in common besides that—which had been all too brief for both of them. And with physical attraction gone and sex life almost nonexistent, there was nothing left between them at all—nothing except the children who tied them almost irrevocably together. *Almost* irrevocably—if only he could earn enough money—

If only they hadn't had children—And yet, of course, he wouldn't put Ellen and Betty back where they'd come from—even if that were possible—now that he had them and loved them.

But damn, damn. Vi, he had seen within two years of marrying her, was incurably stupid, almost aggressively stupid and dull. Nothing, almost literally nothing, could penetrate the carapace of her indifference to everything worthwhile in literature, art, music, living. Nothing above the level of sheer unendurable trash. Love pulps, soap operas, cloying popular ballads—she chewed them all contentedly as a cow chews a cud. She needed, wanted, nothing more; these things were her life, these things and drinking and the eternal eating of candy—box after box of it—that had put forty pounds of weight on her since their marriage, forty flabby pounds that made her body, once slender and desirable, almost as gross and bovine as her mind.

He tried to forget about her and the fact that within four days now she'd be out here with him. He washed the dishes and utensils he had used, put them away, straightened the house again. He liked neatness, orderliness, simplicity, and for a few days more he could have them.

He studied again the three pictures Nelson had left behind him, envying the conception and the execution of each of them. Probably only someone slightly off the beam, like himself, would appreciate them. But he'd give a lot to be able to do a fraction as well.

He decided he might as well take them in today, when he drove in to Taos later for his dinner date, and leave them at a framer's. It would be better if he had them back, already hung, when Vi came. She'd probably never even notice them if they were already on the wall. Otherwise he'd have to explain, and even so she'd think he was crazy to have paid for the framing of such horrible things. He looked about, wondering where they should be hung, and suddenly an idea came to him.

The shed where he'd found them—why couldn't the junk in it be carted away and the place itself cleaned up? Then he could convert it into a studio for himself, a place where he could spend time by himself. The three small rooms of the house—without even a door between two of them—offered almost no privacy at all.

But why couldn't the shed be made into a den, a retreat, a studio, a sanctum? He could keep his paints there, and his books and magazines, and wine—and he could be alone there as much as he wanted. Vi wouldn't understand completely but she would make no objection. And there'd be enough wall space to hang all three of the Nelson canvases; he could have them all to himself.

The thought cheered him tremendously; it was an inspiration that made the summer ahead look infinitely less bleak and boring.

He went out to the shed immediately and looked it over. Yes, it was plenty big enough, about twelve by fourteen. There was a window—with the glass broken—and it was on the side away from the house. The roof didn't seem to leak and the walls were sound except for a knothole or two it would be easy to plug or cover. No electricity, but it wouldn't cost much to run a pair of wires from the house twenty yards away. A small oil burner—he could probably, especially at this season of the year, pick up a used one for a few dollars—would keep it warm on cool evenings. The whole setup would cost him only a few dollars and would be worth hundreds. He could keep his typewriter here, too—

The more he thought of it the more enthusiastic he became; it was the answer to most of the problems that had worried him—particularly the problem of Vi's radio. Vi wouldn't be happy without one, and the interminable programs of soap opera and cheap music would drive him mad if he had to listen to them twelve hours or so a day. Those radio programs had been one of the causes—and not an unimportant cause—of what had happened to him; they'd driven him out of the house, evening after evening, to work or to drink. He simply couldn't stand them, and yet he hated to be brutal with Vi about them because they were such a ridiculously important part of her life.

Would the shed be too dark? No, not if he got himself some flat paint—or maybe even whitewash would do—and painted the walls a light color. And among the junk, that table, if painted and the wobbly leg braced, would do for his typewriter. He could spare one comfortable chair from the house—

Yes, by all means—and before Vi came.

He checked over the items of junk again and found nothing worth salvaging except the table. He measured the window so he could tell Ellis DeLong what size pane to bring. He checked the lock on the door and found that it worked, although it needed oiling.

He drove in to Taos feeling more contented than he'd felt for a long time. He left the three canvases at a frame shop, with orders to frame them as inexpensively as possible, and then went to see Ellis DeLong.

The sunlight was bright and warm and the world was a good place. His thoughts were a long way from murder, murder past or murder yet to come. He didn't think once of Jenny Ames.

But he remembered his date with Carlotta Evers; after he'd made arrangements with DeLong to do the few things the shed required, and as soon as possible, he killed time over a bottle of ale at the Taos Inn until time to pick her up at her apartment near the Harwood.

They ate wiener schnitzel, a specialty of the house, at La Doña Luz. Carlotta was loquacious, but her conversation tended to wander; he had to keep gently leading her back to the topic of Jenny Ames.

"It was so long ago," she almost wailed. "Six or seven years. How can I remember—"

"Eight years, Miss Evers." Weaver turned on his most charming smile. "Yes, a long time, I'll admit. But can't you remember any more than that?"

"I could have, I guess—if I'd known at the time, or even right after, that it was anything worth remembering. But it wasn't until months after that ride on the bus that I knew it was important—I mean that her body was found and I remembered that the girl I'd talked to had been going to meet Mr. Nelson and so she must be the one I talked to. That sounds mixed up, I guess, but you know what I mean. And after two months I couldn't remember *everything* she said, because I wasn't paying an awful lot of attention at the time. You know how it is when you talk to somebody on a bus; it goes in one ear and out the other, except interesting things like that she was coming to Taos to get married and everything."

"But she promised to look you up, you said, after she was married. Didn't you wonder when you didn't hear from her?"

"After seeing her just that once? Of course not. People always promise things like that and how often do they really do them? And then a week or two later I happened to hear that Mr. Nelson had left and I thought they'd just decided to move away and live somewhere else. But then when they found her body, that was different. I tried then to remember everything I could, and the sheriff helped me. He kept asking me questions for hours. And now you're—" The gold tooth flashed. "Well, I guess this dinner is worth it. Go ahead."

"Attagirl," Weaver said. "Then let's start over again—forgive me—at the beginning. You hadn't seen her in the bus station in Santa Fe before you boarded the bus?"

"No, I was almost late for the bus; it was ten minutes after the time it was supposed to leave when I got there, but you know how buses are, always a little late pulling out, so I made it, just barely. I got on just before it started and all the seats were taken except one so I sat down there, and it happened to be the one next to *her*."

"Do you remember what your first impression of her was?"

"I'm afraid I don't, Mr. Weaver. I remember what my impression of her was after the trip, but not what I thought when I first saw her. Probably just that she was pretty, nice-looking, something like that."

"Which of you spoke first?"

"I probably asked her if the seat was taken. You generally do before you sit down beside somebody on a bus." She paused and considered. "I think it was the third or fourth seat back, on the driver's side. And then, just naturally, we got to talking. Probably one of us said it was a beautiful day—it really was—or something like that; that's the way most conversations start. Pretty soon, it couldn't have been more than a minute or two, she asked me how far I was going on the bus—it goes all the way through to Denver, you know, not just to Taos—and I said Taos, and that's when she got really interested. She said she was going to Taos too and that she'd never been there before and would I tell her something about it.

"So I did and she kept asking questions and I guess I was telling her about Taos all the way to Española before I asked her anything about herself; I finally asked her if she was going there on vacation or to take a job or what, and she told me she was going there to marry Charles Nelson and did I know him."

"And did you?"

"I knew who he was, by sight. In a place like this, and eight years ago it wasn't even as big as it is now, you get to know who almost everybody is, even if you don't *know* them."

"How much did you know about Nelson?"

"Only that he was supposed to be an artist and lived out near Seco, and that he wasn't very sociable and hadn't made any friends here. That's about all."

"According to the newspaper account I read, Jenny Ames thought that Nelson taught at one of the art schools here. Did you tell her she was wrong about that?"

"No, because I wasn't *sure* he didn't. I mean, from the little I knew about him, I didn't think he worked for anybody but I wasn't positive about it.",

Weaver nodded. They'd finished dinner by then and were drinking their coffee. "Just think back, Miss Evers. Try to remember if she said anything at all that would give you even a slight clue to where she came from or give what she'd been doing."

"Well—that's what the sheriff kept asking me, but if she said anything about that, I don't remember—I couldn't remember when he was asking me then, so how could I now? I don't think she said anything at all about herself—her past or where she came from, I mean. She was so interested and excited about where she was going and what she was going to do that the other just didn't come up at all."

"But little things, if you can remember them, may have been clues. Did she, for instance, seem familiar with Spanish-Americans or was she curious about them and what they were like?"

"I don't remember her asking about them. But I don't

think she was from New Mexico anywhere. No, don't ask me what it was she said that made me think that—I just remember that I thought it, but I don't know why. And she didn't have any special accent, if you know what I mean. I mean like an Eastern accent or a Texas accent—those I can always tell. Nor Southern. She talked just like most people."

"And what did she tell you about how she met Nelson?"

"That she'd started corresponding with him through a Lonely Hearts Club in some magazine—she didn't say what magazine, I'm sure, or the exact name of the club. That the letters he wrote were wonderful and that after they'd both written awhile, he came for a vacation to the town she lived in and—"

"Did she say *town?* Are you sure of that?"

"I think so, yes. She said that he was there a week and they'd fallen in love with one another but that he had to go back to Taos on account of his job there and they'd arranged for her to follow him as soon as she could get ready, and they were going to get married here. She thought he was awfully handsome and wonderful—I guess any girl thinks that about a man she's going to marry."

It wasn't pay dirt, Weaver was beginning to realize. Except for irrelevant little things such as the sequence of conversation, he hadn't learned anything he hadn't already known.

He tried a different tack. "Can you describe her?"

"Well—no better than I did for the sheriff. She had on a light summer coat, tan, I think. And a hat, but I don't remember what kind. Maybe it was a tam. She was—oh, medium height and weight, kind of a nice figure as far as you could tell with her wearing a coat—and a kind of a pretty face, some make-up but not too much. Dark hair, I didn't remember whether it was black or dark brown, but it turned out that it was black. And—well, that's about all, except that she seemed awfully eager and excited. But she thought she was coming here to get married, so you can't blame her for that."

Weaver didn't blame her for that.

He blamed Carlotta Evers for not remembering the name of the town Jenny Ames had probably mentioned, and for being so vague about everything else—but, he told himself, eight years was eight years and he probably wouldn't do any better himself. He wondered why he'd expected to get anything out of Carlotta now that the sheriff hadn't been able to get out of her only two months after the murder.

He tried a few more times, from a few other angles and with the help of a few post-dinner drinks, and then gave up. He took Carlotta Evers home to her apartment, and made no passes.

He felt that he didn't want to drink wine after the several highballs he'd had after dinner with Carlotta so he picked up a bottle of whisky at a liquor store which was still open on the plaza and took it home with him.

He made himself a drink, a fairly stiff one, and sat in the kitchen sipping it and thinking back over his conversation with Carlotta, wondering if he could deduce from anything she had said any fact, however slight, that he hadn't already known about Jenny Ames.

No, nothing—unless that she seemed more real, more vivid, now that he'd actually talked to someone who had talked to her. But still no clue to where she'd come from, what she'd been.

*Why weren't you missed, Jenny? Why did no word come from whoever knew you after your name was in the papers all over the country? Did you come from Mars or Venus? No, Nelson couldn't have written you there; the mail service is too poor. But why didn't somebody miss you, somewhere? You were lonely, yes, or you'd never have written to a Lonely Hearts Club, but you must have had relatives or at least acquaintances who should have recognized your name.*

Somehow, he thought, it made her seem more pathetic— what happened to her more tragic—that no one knew her. That no one besides the murderer, who had made his getaway, knew whence she came or what she had been. That, besides the murderer, only two people remembered having seen her at all, and one of those two had seen her only for seconds, through a window and from a distance.

*You were cheated out of your life, Jenny, before you had a chance to live it. Quite probably you were a virgin, inexperienced in love. Other men had made advances—they must have if you were pretty, as Pepe and Carlotta say you were—but no one you liked had asked you to marry him and that was what you were waiting for, and you were lonely. So lonely that you wrote to a correspondence club.*

*And hit the jackpot—you thought. A man who corresponded with you and then came to your town to see you. And he was handsome and said he loved you and you loved him, and he said he wanted to marry you. You must have been awfully happy, Jenny, on that bus ride to Taos.*

*But why, Jenny, did he kill you?*

*Was he mad, or was there another reason? Was he Bluebeard, and did you open his closet, perhaps, and see the murdered bodies of his other wives? Then turn, to see him picking up the knife?*

*Damn him,* Weaver thought; *mad or sane I'd like to find him and kill him with my own hands.*

He went to the back door and opened it, stood there staring out into the darkness, listening to the far yapping of the coyotes. He told himself: this happened eight years ago. It doesn't matter now.

The next day, seventy degrees at ten o'clock, humidity negligible, sunshine perfect.

A man of DeLong's came out with a truck; he cleared the junk out of the shed, fixed the broken pane, ran wiring from the meter back of the house and rigged a light in the shed. "I brought the paint, Mr. Weaver," he said. "But Ellis said maybe you wanted to do the painting yourself. That right?"

"That's right. Bring brushes?"

"A three-inch brush, yes. And enough paint to do inside and outside—or did you just want to do the inside?"

Weaver decided that since the paint was here, he might as well paint the outside too.

It was the best day he'd had yet. Something to do, something constructive that would give him the privacy he'd want after Vi's arrival. He got buckets of water from the creek and washed the wooden floor of the shed first, then painted the ceiling and the walls while the floor dried. He painted the floor then and was about to start on the outside when he realized it was mid-afternoon and he was hungry; he hadn't eaten anything since an early breakfast.

**71**

He drove in to Taos to eat so he could pick up the framed pictures if they were ready for him; they were. He ate quickly and hurried back; he got almost half of the outside painted before darkness stopped him.

He slept well that night, dead tired. He finished painting the outside the next morning; the inside was almost dry by then and he decided it would serve without a second coat. He drove in to Taos and found a small used oil heater, some boards for shelving, an army cot. He bought a few tools and some nails to go with the shelving. He'd want a drape of some kind for the window, but that could wait until Vi got here; that was a woman's job.

He checked the post office for mail—there wasn't any—but didn't stop in Taos to eat or to have a drink. He hurried back to finish and furnish his sanctuary. He finished it before dark, and it was good.

Again he got to bed early and slept well. He awoke at dawn and it was Saturday and he lay in bed trying to decide whether he should go to Santa Fe today and spend the night at a hotel there, or whether he should stay here until three or four o'clock in the morning, time to drive down there and pick up Vi. He damned her again for taking such a train when others were available; she wouldn't be leaving Kansas City until this afternoon, maybe he could still send her a telegram telling her to take the bus at Santa Fe and that he'd meet her in Taos. But no, he should have done that right away instead of promising to meet her and then reneging at the last minute.

If he was going to drive down in the early morning, he realized, he'd have to buy an alarm clock today. It was that thought that decided him; an alarm clock would cost as much as a night in a hotel and he certainly had no other use for one, here in Taos. Yes, he'd drive to Santa Fe today and stay there overnight. A call left at the desk would get him waked in time to meet Vi. Also, in Santa Fe it would be easier to find out whether six o'clock was the time the train pulled into Lamy or the time its connecting bus reached Santa Fe.

While he made and drank coffee he found himself wondering what he could do today; no point in driving to Santa

Fe until late afternoon or early evening. Maybe there was some loose end to the Jenny Ames story that he could wind up, and then, as soon as he got his typewriter tomorrow, he could get the thing off to Luke.

But what angle was left that he hadn't tried? Well, there was the hotel in Albuquerque where Jenny had stayed overnight, the night before her fatal trip to Taos. Why not check there? Albuquerque is only sixty-odd miles past Santa Fe; if he left by noon he could drive there today, do his checking, and get back to Santa Fe in the evening. But the paper hadn't mentioned the name of the hotel. Would Callahan remember it, or be able to find out for him?

He killed part of the morning straightening up the house so it would be in perfect order when Vi got there—not that it would stay that way long unless he wanted to keep on doing the work himself—and putting a few finishing touches on the shed. Then he drove to Taos and went to the office of *El Crepúsculo*.

Callahan's desk—an ancient roll-top—was closed and the girl behind the counter said, "Mr. Callahan doesn't come in on Saturdays, sir. But he happens to be in town; he was in here for a minute just a few minutes ago. If you walk around the plaza you'll probably find him somewhere."

Weaver walked around the plaza, looking in at likely places; he found Callahan having a cup of coffee at the counter in the Rio Grande Drugstore. Callahan said, "Hi, Weaver. Cup of coffee? Jeanette! Bring another cup of coffee."

While they drank their coffee, Callahan said, "How goes it with Jenny, Weaver? Get anything from Carlotta?"

"Not much. Guess I've got about all there is to get. There's one angle I might still try, though, if you can help me. I'm driving down to Santa Fe today anyway; I might go on to Albuquerque while I'm at it and see if I can get anything at the hotel she stayed at there. Do you remember the name of it?"

"Ummm, no. Wasn't it in the news story?"

"Pretty positive it wasn't. I made notes of all names and dates and if the hotel had been there, I'd have noted it down."

"Let me think awhile. It may come to me. You're not in a hurry to leave, are you?"

"No."

"Not that I think you'll get anything important there. You know, the more you think about that case—and you've got me thinking about at lately—the funnier it gets. No beginning and no end—nothing except what happened here. We don't know where Nelson came from—unless the Colorado license plates on his car meant he came from there and I doubt it—nor where he went, outside of that one stop in Amarillo. We don't know where the Ames girl came from, beyond that one night in Albuquerque. We don't know—we don't know much of anything."

"Did they trace the license number on Nelson's car?"

"Would have if anybody had noticed it or remembered it. But nobody did. Like your car—I've seen it and noticed that it's a Missouri license, but I don't remember the number."

"Not sure I remember it myself. I see what you mean. Listen, you say Sheriff Freeman's dead, but what about any deputies of his who may have worked on the case? Would any of them be around?"

"Afraid not. Freeman had only two deputies. One of them went into the army shortly after that; I don't know what happened to him except that he never came back to Taos. The other—let's see—he got a job with the state police a couple of years ago, but the last I heard he was working in the southern part of the state, around Lordsburg, hell of a ways from here. You might find him, but I doubt if it would be worth the trouble. Joe Sandoval his name is; he did some leg work on the case, but he's no mental heavyweight. Hey, I just thought how you can get the name of that Albuquerque hotel."

"How?"

"At the *Albuquerque Tribune*; they'll have it in their files. They covered the case—even had a reporter up here for the inquest. And to them the fact that she'd spent the night before she was killed at a hotel there is a local angle; their stories would be sure to play it up—probably with an interview with the desk clerk who'd registered her, if he remembered her at all."

"Thanks. Silly of me not to have thought of that myself."

Callahan laughed. "Sillier of *me*—as a newspaperman—not to have thought of it sooner. Well, I'd better push along; got some errands to do yet and want to get home by noon. Have a good trip."

It was a good trip. The road from Taos to Santa Fe and thence to Albuquerque goes through some spectacular and breathtaking country, and it is at its best in early June.

Weaver thought it strange, but not too strange, that as he drove through the narrow, tortuous streets of Santa Fe—streets laid out for burro traffic rather than for automobiles—he had no desire to look up any of the people he knew there. Had known, rather. Why, now, try to renew contacts that meant nothing to him any longer? The past was gone—like Jenny Ames was gone. White bones by now, crumbling. Where? He'd never thought to ask. Unless for a photograph to accompany the story, what did it matter? No, he didn't want to see Jenny's grave. He'd always hated the thought of graves and cemeteries; he'd never gone to visit the graves of his own parents. Not because he was above sentiment, or below it, but because it had seemed such a useless, even a ridiculous gesture. As though the dead knew whether you came to visit their graves or not.

The way to visit the dead is the approach of one's mind to their memory, not the approach of one's body to their graves.

It was hot in Albuquerque when he arrived there in midafternoon, enough to make him appreciate the mountain mildness of Taos summer. And Albuquerque had grown greatly in size since he'd last seen it. There'd been only a slight difference in Santa Fe, but Albuquerque seemed almost twice the size it had been when he'd last seen it five years before. It had been a large town then; it was a small city now.

He found a place to park near the *Albuquerque Tribune* office. He went in and explained what he wanted to a young man who came to the desk. A few minutes later he was looking through a bound volume of papers eight years old. He started with July 15th, the day the body had been found; the story hadn't reached Albuquerque in time to make the paper that day.

The next issue had a full column—and Callahan had been right; the local angle was played up. A fair portion of the story—and the rest of it included nothing that hadn't been in the Taos paper—was devoted to the fact that Jenny Ames had spent the night before her death, the night of May 16th, at the Colfax Hotel in Albuquerque, that she had undoubtedly taken the eleven o'clock bus the following morning for Santa Fe.

There was an interview with the clerk at the Colfax Hotel, Ward Haver by name, but little was brought out except the fact that he remembered the girl but vaguely; that she had checked in, according to the records, at four o'clock in the afternoon and had checked out at ten-thirty the following morning. She'd stayed in Room 36.

Weaver read the rest of the story and skimmed through the papers following; nothing further that was new to him. He closed the bound volume; the young man who had brought it to him came back to the desk and Weaver asked him, "Your current editor—did he hold the job eight years ago?"

"Mr. Carson? I'm not sure; I know he's been with the paper quite a while, but I've been here only two years myself. Shall I ask him?"

"Well—I'd like to see him in any case. If he wasn't here then, he'll probably know who to refer me to. My name's Weaver, George Weaver."

"Just a moment, Mr. Weaver."

Then he was being shown through a door into a private office and a man with thinning gray hair said, "Yes. Mr. Weaver? I'm Carson."

"Were you editor here at the time of the Jenny Ames murder near Taos, eight years ago?"

"I wasn't editor then, but I worked here. Worked on the case, in fact."

"You were the man who was sent to Taos to cover the inquest?"

"No, that was Tommy Mainwarren; he isn't here any more. But I covered the local angle, the hotel and the depots and whatnot."

"Good, that's what I'm interested in right now." Weaver explained briefly why he was interested. "Do you have a few minutes to spare?"

"A few, yes. Just what do you want to know?"

"Well, this occurred to me while I was reading your story just now, in the outer office. How was it learned so quickly that Jenny Ames had stayed here at the Colfax Hotel? I assumed that the clerk had probably read a news story and had remembered the name—but the hotel angle was in the first story you ran, so it couldn't have been that."

"Let's see—we first learned about the story when our regular Taos correspondent, whoever it may have been then—I don't remember, phoned us a tip on the story. It looked like a big story so Tommy Mainwarren was sent up there right away to cover it. When he phoned in the story I took it down. That happened to be several hours before press time and I got to thinking about the fact that she'd taken the one o'clock bus out of Santa Fe. That bus leaves Albuquerque around eleven and she might have come from here. I asked Henderson—he was the editor then—if I could check that angle and he told me to go ahead.

"I trotted down to the bus depot and tried to get something—but I couldn't. Nobody remembered after two months—and you can't blame them for that with only a pretty general description—anything about the girl. Be funny, for that matter, if anybody had. You don't have to give your name to buy a bus ticket and unless you do something unusual—like spitting in the ticket seller's eye or breaking a window in the bus while you're riding it—nobody's going to remember you after two months. None of the ticket sellers who'd been working that day remembered her, nor did the driver who'd had that run—I was lucky enough to catch him at the station."

The editor struck a match under his desk and pulled fire into an ancient pipe. "But the local angle was still worth trying for and it hit me that she might have stayed over in a hotel here if she had come through this way, so I phoned hotels and asked them to check their registrations for the name Jenny Ames on—whatever night it would have been. Hit pay dirt at the Colfax."

Weaver nodded. "That was good work. And—well, I just read the story you wrote so I guess I know what you found out. The clerk remembered her, but not very well."

"He was barely sure that he remembered her at all. If we'd had a picture of her to refresh his memory we might have got more. But the records showed when she checked in and when she checked out—just in time to get that eleven o'clock bus to Santa Fe, so there's no doubt she was on it even if they don't remember her. And the clerk thinks he remembers she had two suitcases. I guess the story contained the fact that she put Taos as her address on the registration card?"

"Yes."

"Logical enough," Carson said, "although too bad she figured it that way. She must have thought that was going to be her permanent address and she might as well start using it instead of an obsolete address she didn't intend to return to. Anything else?" He stared at the ceiling a few seconds. "Oh, yes, I tried to see how she came into Albuquerque the day before. She checked in at the hotel some time late in the afternoon—"

"Four o'clock, according to the story."

"That's right, four o'clock. I checked arrival times of trains and buses; no train came in for several hours before then. But there was a bus arrival at three-thirty. And anyway, since she stayed at the Colfax, it's more likely she came in by bus. The Colfax was just across the street from the bus terminal and half a block down; you see the sign as you come out of the door and it's a natural thing, if you're a stranger in town, to head for the nearest hotel if there's one in sight.

"I checked some more at the bus terminal and couldn't get any proof that she had really come in on that bus, but it seems likely. Especially when I found it had been twenty minutes late that day; got in at ten minutes of four. Allowing ten minutes for her to get her bags if she'd checked them through and to cross the street and walk half a block, that'd make the four o'clock check-in time at the Colfax just right."

Weaver nodded. "You used the past tense about the Colfax Hotel," he said. "Isn't it there any more?"

"No, it was razed several years ago to make room for a big office building. It was a small hotel—only three stories."

"And the clerk, Ward Haver?"

"Haven't an idea. I didn't know him, outside of that one talk with him."

"The three-thirty bus that she probably came in on. What was its route?"

"Los Angeles-Phoenix-Globe-Socorro. That run. The police tried to trace her back along it to find her starting point, but they didn't get anywhere. Be a miracle, I suppose, if they had, after that length of time. Well, Mr. Weaver, I'm afraid that's all I can tell you."

Weaver thanked him and left.

He looked in an Albuquerque phone book—on the off-chance—for the name of Ward Haver, and it wasn't there. It didn't really matter; the clerk could scarcely have told him anything he hadn't told Carson. And it would be futile for him to try any checking at the bus terminal; that had been tried eight years ago, and by the police as well as by a reporter, and it hadn't paid off then.

There was nothing further for him in Albuquerque. He drove back to Santa Fe and got there by dinner time.

**V**i gave him a perfunctory smile and then her pasty face went quickly sullen again. "It was an *awful* trip, George. I couldn't sleep a wink all night long. I'm *so* tired. And hungry, too, simply starving. They hadn't opened the dining car yet."

Weaver said, "Come on, we'll find you somewhere to eat. I could use a cup of coffee myself."

"But the *baggage*, George. There's all that stuff you told me to bring, typewriter, bedding, dishes—"

He grinned at her. "They didn't make you carry it, did they? Let's have some breakfast first. We can pick up the luggage afterwards."

Over breakfast—and Vi packed away a big one—Weaver

studied her. She managed to pout, to look sullen, even when she was eating. Her eyes seemed even duller. And she'd gained weight, he was sure, in the few weeks since he'd left Kansas City. He could picture her alone in the apartment there, tippling all afternoon and alternating sips of whisky with chocolate creams while she read confession magazines and listened to interminable radio programs. Probably she hadn't been outdoors once since he left, unless it was to go to a movie in the evening. Spots of rouge on her cheeks were the only color in her face.

What had made her that way, he wondered for possibly the ten thousandth time since their marriage. Had it been his fault?

He didn't see how, basically. In a few little things, yes. He hadn't been perfect by any means. But back in the early days of their marriage, when they'd loved one another, at least physically, he'd tried his best to help her get interested in—well, in worthwhile things. He hadn't nagged her about it; he'd simply, for example, exposed her to good music by taking her places where she could hear it, by buying good records and playing them once in a while. By seeing that there were good books and magazines around the house as well as the ones she bought for herself. Not highbrow stuff either; he tried to settle for educating her up to *Collier's* or the *Post* instead of *Dream Romances* and *Movie Confessions*. And, although he liked symphonies and quartets himself, he'd have settled if she'd liked Crosby or Goodman instead of Texas Slim.

No, her taste had been unchangeable, no matter how hard or how subtly he tried to improve it. All that had changed about her was that, once she'd got herself a man, she'd let herself go, cared little about her appearance and less about her figure. She'd vegetated, sunk into a morass of mushy reading and listening, steady drinking, even steadier eating.

About the only thing he could say for her was that she hadn't been unfaithful to him—or did he know even that? She flirted with other men sometimes, was coy with them, but he'd simply assumed she didn't have the incentive to go farther than that. Maybe he was wrong—but it didn't matter. He might have cared once, but he didn't now. Except for the girls' sake, of course.

How on earth was it that the two girls, born of Vi, had good minds? So keen that even now, at their ages, they must know that their mother was a dipsomaniac. They'd know soon enough if she was or became as sloppy morally as she was in every other way. Maybe after all it would be better to make a clean break—

He shook his head to clear it. No, it simply couldn't be done. Right now, especially, when he wasn't earning a cent, it was utterly ridiculous even to think of such a thing.

He said, "There's egg on your chin, dear."

She wiped it off, absently. "Why didn't you take a place in Santa Fe, George?" She frowned at him. "We don't know *anybody* in Taos."

He grinned. "That's why I picked the place, maybe. You know the doctor's orders, Vi. Peace and seclusion. If it was just a matter of not working, we could have stayed in Kansas City. But wait till you see—"

She was eating again, not listening. And why go on with what he'd started to say? He knew suddenly—and wondered why he hadn't thought of it before—that she wouldn't appreciate mountains and sunshine and beauty. She hadn't liked even Santa Fe, really; it had been at her urging that he'd gone to a bigger city when he'd decided to go in business for himself—choosing Kansas City because he already had a few connections there.

No, Vi wasn't going to like Taos. She was going to like living ten miles outside of Taos, in the last house on a road, even less.

She finished eating and there was egg on her chin again, but he didn't bother telling her about it. This time, though, she took a compact from her purse and looked into the mirror of it; she wiped the egg off before she dabbed her face with the powder puff and then put lipstick—too much of it, of course—on her over-full, petulant lips. She took a comb from her purse.

He said, "Please, Vi."

"Oh, that's right; you don't like it when I use a comb at the table. All right, I'll wait."

She got a cigarette out and he held his lighter for her.

"What time is it, George?"

"A few minutes after seven." He stared past her through the coffee-shop window at the brightening day outside. He wished she'd hurry so they could get going on the drive to Taos. But he'd have to sit here a long time; Vi would want a second cup of coffee and probably a third, and she'd take her time over each of them while a pile of lipstick-smeared cigarette butts grew in the ash tray.

"Do you guess a bar would be open this early, George? I mean, by the time I've had another cup of coffee, I know it seems awful to have a drink this early, but I couldn't *sleep* on the train and I'm so tired that if I had a drink or two I could maybe nap on the way up."

"It's Sunday, Vi. No bars or liquor stores open." He saw her face fall and relented. "But I've got a bottle in the car. You can have a nip as soon as we start."

At least that got her started sooner; she had only a second cup of coffee instead of her usual three.

He got the car from the garage where he'd left it overnight and drove to the railroad office; Vi waited in the car, combing her mousy colored hair with the aid of the rear-vision mirror, while he got the luggage and loaded it into the back of the car.

He waited until they were outside of town and then took the bottle from the glove compartment and handed it to Vi. He didn't want a drink himself, this early.

But he'd long ago given up worrying about Vi's drinking or trying to get her to cut down on it. Once, five years ago, when she'd first shown a tendency toward dipsomania—before then she'd drunk moderately—he'd gone on the wagon for almost a year himself. But Vi's drinking had increased anyway.

She had several nips from the bottle and then, after a while, she dozed, her head falling against his shoulder. Weaver drove carefully to avoid waking her. Thus far she'd asked almost nothing about the place she'd be living in, and he'd told her little in his letters; she wasn't going to like it, he knew. But let her see it first and get the argument all over with at once instead of having to talk about it now and spoil the drive.

They reached Taos by ten o'clock and the house ten miles beyond it twenty minutes later.

Vi didn't like the place. She hated it.

"It gives me the *creeps*, George. Way out here in *nowhere*. No people at all!"

"It's only ten miles to Taos, Vi. Fifteen or twenty minutes in the car. You can make all the friends there that you want. And you can use the car all you wish."

He hoped that she would, even though he worried whenever she drove the car. She wasn't a good driver.

"But, George, it's *awful* after our apartment in Kansas City. It's a dump, that's what it is. A mud hut. And I'm afraid. It gives me the creeps to be way out here. At night—"

"I won't leave you alone here at night. Not that there's anything to be afraid of."

"George, I *won't stay*. An outside toilet! And I *will* be afraid—"

She was almost crying.

Weaver listened patiently. He didn't argue back; he let her get it out of her system. He got her inside and started bringing stuff in from the car. Her radio first—and he plugged it in, turned it on. Let her realize that she'd at least have this—which, anyway, was her main anodyne, more important to her than whisky.

She was sitting sobbing—but listening to the radio—while he brought in the other things. He went out into the kitchen and made them drinks—one for himself this time. He gave her one and sat down with his own.

"Listen, Vi, I'm sorry you dislike it—this much. But it's just for three months. For you, anyway; maybe I'll be staying a little longer but you'll have to go back in three months anyway to get the girls out of camp and into school. And the sublet of the apartment will be over then and you'll have it back. Now be a good sport for that long, huh?"

"But, George—"

"It won't be too bad, Vi. We won't get in one another's hair, even if the place is small. I'm going to be writing and painting and I made that little shed—see it out the back window?—into a studio and workshop for myself. You can play the radio all you want, you can read all the damn magazines you want—and that's what you'd be doing if you were back home, so what's the difference where you do it? And the climate here—well, you're getting a sample right now, and it's like this all summer.

"And besides, I've already got this place paid for, so we can't afford to live anywhere else now."

"All right, all right, all *right*."

The worst was over. He made them each another drink.

She was tired and still sleepy after she drank it and she went into the bedroom to lie down and sleep awhile. After a few minutes George heard her deep breathing and took a deep breath of relief himself.

He walked to the bedroom doorway and stood watching her closely for a minute or two. Strangely, he felt more tenderness, just then, than any other emotion.

Poor Vi; it wasn't really her fault that she was what she was. Their unhappiness was his fault much more than hers. His fault for leaping before he looked, for not having known her long enough, before he suggested marriage, to have realized the complete incompatibility between them.

Poor Vi; she was caught in a trap, even as he. Like him, she acquiesced in a marriage without love because fundamentally she was decent enough to think of the children first. She was weak, silly—but not vicious. Her selfishness was all in little things.

And in one way at least this must be worse for her than for him; she was the more romantic one of the two of them. Love stories, love songs, every form of sentimental mush and gush, were her very life.

He looked down at her closed eyes, her puffy face, her dishwater-colored hair that managed to be stringy despite frequent, and misnamed, permanents. Her skin was getting blotchy from too much drinking and too much candy— he often wondered which was the worse for her. Still under thirty but with her body getting grosser every year, her breasts beginning to be flabby and to sag, striation marks from a difficult delivery marring her thighs, the ugly mole—

Dreaming now, no doubt, of some Prince Charming of a radio program or a magazine story—who, for Vi, would never come. She was stuck with him, George Weaver—and, just for a moment, he saw himself through her eyes.

Let her sleep, for as long as she could.

He took his typewriter out to the shed and put it on the table there, stacked paper next to it.

He sat down in front of it and fed a piece of white paper into the machine, then sat staring at it, wondering how he could begin to write the story of Jenny Ames. Then wondering if he could write it at all.

He'd found out all he could—had talked to everybody who knew anything about her at all, and still he knew absolutely nothing that was not in the newspaper account.

Did it make a story? No, there were too many missing factors. An algebraic equation full of unknowns, and the biggest unknown was Jenny herself.

Picture her, picture her in the horrible moment that Pepe Sanchez had seen. Could he start the story there?

*Sudden terror in her eyes, Jenny backed away from the knife, her hand groping behind her for the knob of the kitchen door. She was too frightened to scream and anyway there was no one to hear, no one but the man who came toward her with the knife—and he was mad, he must be mad. Her hand found the knob and turned it; the door swung outward into the night and she whirled through it, running. Death ran after her.*

But the words wouldn't come. The picture, but not the words.

Damn, he thought; why was he trying this at all? He wasn't a writer. Why didn't he simply send the facts he had, meager or not, to Luke and tell him that was everything available and then let Luke do the rest? Why didn't he simply get it off his mind, the easy way?

After a while he heard the radio from the house; Vi must be awake again. And it was a talking program but not loud enough for him to understand the voices so that was all right. As long as he couldn't make out the words, the sound itself was almost soothing.

Damn it, he ought to write to Luke anyway. And there was paper in the machine; why not now? He put a date line on the paper and then:

Dear Luke:

I'm afraid I'm being frustrated by the job you gave me. I've been digging in, or trying to—but there just aren't any facts I can find out besides those in the newspaper account of the murder. And you must have read that, and decided it was insufficient, when you made your own investigation of the case. In fact, if you took notes at that time and still have them, I don't know how I can help you at all.

There's still that damnable puzzle of the *motive*. Was it purely a psychopathic crime or was there gain for Nelson? If only Jenny Ames could be traced back beyond Albuquerque, maybe we could get somewhere. But if she couldn't be traced then, how can she be traced now, after eight years?

The odd thing is how deeply I've found myself interested, almost obsessed, in thinking about the missing pieces of the puzzle—and how curious I've become.

It occurs to me—just now, in fact—that Nelson *might* have been traced, at the time, through his painting style. He wasn't just pretending to be an artist; maybe he wasn't too good a painter, but he took himself seriously. Wherever he went from here, he kept on painting. I've got three pictures of his—they were in the shed back of the house—that I've had framed because I like them.

His style is quite individual: I think if I ever saw another painting of his—at least one painted at about the same period—I'd recognize it at sight. It's too late now, probably, but if somebody had thought, then, to hang those three pictures somewhere in Taos, say in the lobby of a hotel where tourists would see them, and put a placard by them explaining that a wanted killer had painted them, sooner or later someone would have said, "Why, I know who painted those—"

I also have a hunch, incidentally, that Nelson stayed in the Southwest. It seems probable that he had t.b., although since he wasn't treated by a doctor here nobody knows how badly he had it. But it's probable that he'd want to stay in the warm dry climate of New Mexico or Arizona—probably that's why he came here in the first place. And if he intended to cut back westward again and wanted to throw pursuit off the trail, that would account for why he registered under the name of Nelson in Amarillo, east of here. (There's also sixty dollars worth of reason in the form of cashed traveler's checks.) But I think he might have gone as far east as Amarillo deliberately and established himself there, as it were, on purpose to make the police think he was heading east or south (he left a red herring query about the roads to El Paso) so he could double back to, say, Arizona and not be traced there. The police should have concentrated their search there—particularly in artists' colonies and tuberculosis sanatoriums. Or maybe they did, for all I know; maybe I'm second guessing. But they *did* miss that angle of reproducing his pictures.

I wish I could think of some equivalently good way of trying to trace Jenny Ames backward to wherever she came from.

Well, if you want me to send you what dope I have, let me know and I'll do it. But I don't think it's really enough—and I'm just cussed enough and *interested* enough to keep on trying—if I can think of any more angles to try. Also it gives me something to do and something to be interested in—and God knows I need both.

Vi is here now; got in this morning.

Do you still want me to go ahead and take some pictures to go with the article? Or, unless I get something more on the story itself, should we forget the whole thing? I can take a picture or two of the house—will probably do that anyway—and maybe an interior shot of the kitchen, showing the doorway Pepe Sanchez saw her run through. And if you think

it's worth it, maybe I can find the man who found the
body and have him show me the exact spot so I can
take a picture of that. . . .

He finished the letter and got it ready to mail; then he
went back to the house. Vi was eating candy and listening
to the radio. The radio voices weren't soothing, now that
he could hear them clearly.

"Time for lunch, Vi. Let's celebrate your arrival by eating
in Taos this noon. And it'll give you a chance for a look at
the town; I drove right through it on the way here. Besides,
I've got a letter I want to mail."

"All right, George. But when this program is over.
Shhhhh."

Weaver waited.

**T**ime, a week of it, passed slowly. To Weaver, it seemed
like a month.

He worried about money, for one thing. Money is something to worry about when none is coming in and plenty—
more than he'd anticipated—going out. There was going to
be less left in the fall than he'd hoped. He worried about
how difficult it might be for him to get into the swing of
things; and if there was no backlog left, he'd be starting
cold, from scratch.

The money was going out faster than he'd thought it
would go. Vi's drinking—and she disliked wine, so her
drinking cost more than his—didn't help. And almost every
night she wanted to go, insisted on going, to one of the bars
in Taos. And when you go to a bar you buy drinks for others and it runs you at least ten dollars before the evening is
over, as against less than half that much if you stay home
and do your drinking there. Oh, he enjoyed it—or parts of
it—in a way, but there was the money going. Free rent,
sure, but they were spending overall as much as if they'd
kept their apartment in Kansas City. And, on top of it, the

money that it was taking to keep the two girls in camp. Not that he begrudged that.

So he worried. Sometimes he had dreams, almost nightmares, of the kind that had started his breakdown and had sent him to the sanatorium back home.

He told himself, you damned fool, you're here so you won't worry. Forget it. A month or two without worrying at all is better than a whole goddam summer spent in worrying how much you're spending. Forget money.

Sure, but try to forget money when it's going out and not coming in, and when the bottom of your bank account is in sight and you don't know how soon you'll be working again or how much money you'll be able to make when you are. Try to forget money under circumstances like that.

Well, there's one way. Concentrate away from it. Think about something else.

He concentrated on Jenny Ames just for something to concentrate on. He'd tried to paint and it hadn't helped. He'd tried to write, and he couldn't. Neither fact surprised him; he knew that he was neither a painter nor a writer. He was just a—*what* was he? Just a guy who'd learned a little about the real estate business and didn't know enough to do anything else, and had been forbidden to do the only thing he did know. Not that that worried him—he didn't really *like* real estate—except for the fact that no money was coming in.

He found himself thinking a lot about Jenny Ames.

Of an evening, he'd be sitting in the kitchen having a drink with Vi, while it was early dark, still too early for them to drive into Taos if they were going that night, and he'd catch himself staring at the kitchen door that led out into the night, the illimitable dark into which—

Sometimes he'd sit there again after they'd come home, a little drunk, Vi already in bed (she was always ready to turn in when they returned; Weaver seldom was) and—well, he'd almost see Jenny standing there. A girl with a white face and black hair, a green dress, her hand groping behind her for the door.

Once, when he was drunk enough, he talked to her. But she didn't answer.

It was the day after that when he began to find himself hating the three Nelson paintings hanging in his shack. Oh, he still liked them, but now he hated them too. And that happened to be the day he got a letter from Luke about the paintings. It read:

Dear George:
  You idiot, you. You write and ask me whether it's worth while carrying on writing a story about the Jenny Ames murder and you almost convince me, for the first umpteen paragraphs, that it isn't, and then you come up with an idea that's worth its weight in printer's ink.
  There probably ought to be a special law in artists' colonies like Taos that sheriffs and other law officers ought to have a working knowledge of art. Then the sheriff who worked on the Nelson case wouldn't have overlooked, while it was hot, the idea of circularizing the country to find Nelson through his painting style.
  Now after eight years, it's pretty much of an off-chance that he can be found that way. *But*, you idiot, don't you see that whether it works or not isn't the important thing. The important thing is that now you've got a really good story angle, so good that selling the story is a lead-pipe cinch. And you ask if pictures of the paintings should be taken!
  That's your lead. The fact that now, through this article, an eight-year old murder may be solved through an angle that was overlooked at the time of the original investigation. "Does any reader of this article know an artist who paints, or who painted eight years ago, in the style of the three pictures shown here?"
  It's a dilly, George. That's the peg on which you hang the whole thing. Guard those pictures, and that idea, with your life. See that nobody beats you to the punch on it.
  I still don't see why somebody didn't think of it at the time—unless the sheriff was the only one who

knew about them. That could have been; I didn't learn about them in the course of the brief investigation I made of the case, and I probably would have if their existence had been general knowledge.

But those pictures are a real find, and they make the story money in the bank for you if you handle it right. It makes it so damn good that I hate to cut in on it. Why don't you write it yourself, George?

There are two good reasons why you should. One is that I've got an extension of my contract here; I've been hired to work on two more crime documentaries after this one. I'm making more money than I've ever made before and—hold thumbs for me—if the pictures I'm working on go over, I might never have to go back to magazine writing at all. The other reason is that the idea and the discovery of the paintings is strictly yours and I've got no business to chisel in, even if I needed dough, which I don't.

So let's change my original suggestion to this: You write the article and take the photographs, including really good ones of the paintings, and send them to me. If the article turns out to be salable as written I'll forward it to my agent in New York to peddle for you and won't cut in at all. Counting the price you'll get for the photographs, and counting out the agent's fee of ten percent, you should get at least three hundred, maybe four hundred bucks.

If your story needs rewriting—and it shouldn't if you read a couple of fact detective magazines to get the general style and slant—I'll rewrite it for you. If all the data is there, no matter how you've written it, it shouldn't be more than a couple of hours work for me, and the charge will be one bottle of whisky, payable after you've made the sale and whenever we'll have a chance to drink it together. It's got to be good whisky—I'm acquiring expensive habits out here in Hollywood—but it won't make too big a hole in your profits on the deal.

Glad to learn that Vi is now with you and that . . .

Three or four hundred bucks, Weaver thought. That much money was worth shooting for. And he'd been thinking of trying to write the story himself anyway.

"Vi, did you bring my camera?"

"Camera? Oh, George, I *forgot* about it. I remember now your writing me to bring it, same time you told me to bring the typewriter, but the camera was put away in the trunk I'd already sent to storage, the things we didn't want to leave in the apartment while it was sublet, and I was going to go down to the storage company and get it and then at the last minute there were so many things to do and . . ."

"That's all right, Vi. I want to take a few pictures while we're here, but I can rent or borrow a camera for a few days. Want to ride in with me now? You can have a drink while I'm hunting one up. There's a photographer's place near the Taos Inn; I can probably get one there."

"Sure, George. But I can't go dressed *this* way—"

They left half an hour later, Vi dressed another way, and drove to Taos. He left Vi at the Taos Inn sipping a martini—her favorite drink in bars, although it was too much trouble for her to make them for herself when she drank at home—while he made arrangements to rent a camera for a few days and bought several rolls of film to go with it.

He'd get right at taking the pictures, he decided, and he'd start work right away on the story. Three or four hundred bucks would make a hell of a lot of difference in his budget. He knew that he was taking advantage of Luke's generosity to take him up on the proposition, especially if it turned out that Luke would really have to rewrite the story, but maybe he could make it up to Luke some time, some way.

Let's see, was there anything else he wanted before starting the story?

Before he went into the bar of the Taos Inn to get Vi, he went to the phone in the lobby and called Callahan.

"Weaver," he said. "Callahan, do you know whether the Seco man who found the body is still around? If I remember the name right, it's Ramon Camillo."

"That's the name, but I don't know if he's still around or not. Ask them at the Arroyo Seco post office; they'll be able to tell you—and to tell you where he lives, if he's still there."

"Thanks, I'll do that."

"Find out what you wanted to find out in Albuquerque?"

"More or less. The hotel's gone, but I talked to the editor of the *Tribune* and got a few little extra details that'll help the story."

"Good. Say, Weaver, I understand your wife's with you now. Why don't you drop around at the house with her some time? Do you play bridge?"

"I do, but the missus doesn't. Sorry."

"Well, bridge isn't the only thing in the world. Drop around anyway—any evening; if our lights are on, we're home."

Weaver promised that they would.

He wondered whether he meant it or not. He liked Callahan all right, but he'd rather meet Mrs. Callahan first before he brought Vi around. Vi was—well, Vi could be embarrassing when she drank too much, and she'd probably drink too much if drinks were served. And if Callahan's wife was the dignified, reserved type of woman, she'd be embarrassed by Vi. Vi seldom got bitchy from drinking—although even that could happen—but four or five drinks could make her pretty sloppy, and that was almost as bad.

Bridge. He wished that they could play bridge. He'd liked it a lot, once. And he'd tried his best to teach Vi to play, but she just·didn't have the brains to learn, or sufficient ability to concentrate. After a year of trying, her bidding and playing were so random and haphazard that—for the sake of the people they'd tried to play with—he'd given up the game completely.

He got Vi out of the bar and drove toward home, stopping at the little post office in Arroyo Seco en route. He asked the postmaster about Ramon Camillo.

"Ramon,. he still lives here winters. But summers up in Colorado, Montana, the sheep."

Weaver started to ask whether anybody in Seco besides Camillo would know the exact spot where Jenny Ames' body had been found and then he realized Sanchez would be able to tell him that—and that if he asked Sanchez he wouldn't have to go through the rigmarole of explaining all over again what his interest was.

He thanked the postmaster and drove on to Sanchez's house.

Sanchez opened the door and smiled; he stepped back. "Please to come in, Mr. Weaver?"

"Thanks, no. My wife is waiting in the car and I just want to ask you one question. Is there someone in Seco who knows the exact place where Jenny Ames' body was found and who could take me there and show me?"

"You not need somebody to show you, Mister Weaver. I tell you how you find yourself the place. From your house a quarter mile straight north is cottonwood, big cottonwood, bigger than any tree near. By it, you can see the place. You find easy."

Weaver thanked him and drove on home. It was still only mid-afternoon and a quarter of a mile wasn't far to walk. He loaded the camera and started out, walking straight north. Just beyond the shed he turned back a moment, thinking that he should have asked Vi if she wanted to go along for a walk. Then he decided against it; he didn't want her along because he didn't want to explain what he was doing. He hadn't discussed the Jenny Ames case with her—and was reluctant to do so.

He didn't know exactly why he felt almost revolted at even the thought of mentioning Jenny Ames' name to Vi, but he did feel that way. And anyway there was a very practical reason for keeping his own counsel—the money. If Vi knew of the very excellent chance of three or four hundred dollars coming in, she'd be even more careless of money for the rest of the summer than she'd be otherwise.

So let Vi think he was walking back just to photograph the mountains. For that matter, he might as well take some shots of them too. He had plenty of film and, in any case, he'd have to take some pictures he could show Vi later to account for his having rented the camera. Pictures he took of the house itself could do double duty in that respect and he could take them any time, whether Vi was around or not. He'd have to wait until sometime when she was away from the house to take his shots of the paintings.

He started to pace off the distance roughly; at a yard to a stride a quarter of a mile would be about four hundred and forty paces. He counted up to three hundred and then, as he topped a rise, he knew he could quit counting; the cottonwood tree ahead of him, halfway up the next slope, was the one. There was no mistaking it; it was the biggest tree anywhere in sight and the distance and direction were just about what Sanchez had told him. He headed for it with certainty.

Had Jenny Ames, he wondered, actually run that far before the killer had caught up to her? Or had he caught her sooner and then carried her body farther away from the house before he buried it?

Yes, this was the tree. For there, just under and beyond it, was the depression that had once been a shallow grave. Now weathered to a depth of only about six inches, it was still unmistakably discernible.

He photographed it from several angles, not knowing from which side it would show up best in a photograph. He took a few shots of the mountains, too.

The sun was still warm and bright as he walked back to the house. Might as well photograph it now too, and finish one roll of film.

He backed his car out to the road so it wouldn't be in the picture and then took three shots of the house from three different distances and angles. One of them from the exact spot where Pepe Sanchez had stood. That, no doubt, would be the one they'd use, but it didn't hurt to have other pictures for them to choose among.

The interior shot—and he'd have to make several tries on that, with different time exposures on each so one of them would come out—would have to wait until Vi was away. Too difficult to explain, otherwise.

But come to think of it, he had a perfectly logical excuse for taking pictures of the paintings, if Vi should notice what he was doing and become curious. He could tell her he was just experimenting on how to photograph pictures because, later, he'd want to photograph some of his own water colors, and if he knew the right distance and exposure, he wouldn't have any misses when he tried that.

That made sense as an explanation. Enough for Vi, anyway.

He took the pictures from the shed and stood them against the west wall so the afternoon sun would be squarely on them. He shortened the tripod so the camera would be about on center of the pictures and then moved it back and forth until he had the distance just right so the picture would fill the field, set his focus and took the shots. Just one of each of the three pictures; if they didn't come out well the first time he'd try again after he knew whether he'd over- or underexposed.

Vi came out while he was taking the final shot.

"George do you *like* those horrible things? I can't see how you can *stand* them hanging in that shed of yours. And you spend so much time in it, too."

He snapped the camera. "Well, they're interesting, Vi. I don't exactly like them, but I wish I could do as well. And the more you look at them, the more you see in them. But—" And he explained that, really, he was just experimenting with the camera, that he'd never tried to take a picture of a picture before.

Weaver took the three pictures back into the shed and hung them again, closing the door so he couldn't hear Vi's radio. He checked the camera and found there was one frame left on the second roll of film. He filled it with a random shot of mountains framed by the window of his shed and then took the film out. He looked at his watch. Just barely time to get them to the photographer's by five o'clock if he left right away.

He went into the house and turned the radio down a little so he could be heard. "Going into town, Vi, to leave these films. Any shopping you want done?"

"Well—you could get some bread and something for sandwiches if it's all right to have that tonight. I'd rather not cook another hot meal."

"Okay."

"And some whisky, George, and some ginger ale. There's only half a bottle left. I was going to remember it when we were in before, and I forgot."

The photograph shop told him the pictures would be finished day after next. He ordered only contact prints, one of each, until he had a chance to see how they'd turn out.

He got the whisky and the ginger ale, some wine for himself, the bread and sandwich meat.

It was dusk when he returned and Vi said she was hungry so they ate right away.

"George, let's go to a movie tonight. I haven't seen a movie since I came here."

He sighed. "I've got a slight headache, Vi. Why don't you take the car and drive in yourself? Anyway, it's a gangster movie; I happened to notice. You like them and I don't."

When she'd left, half an hour later, the house seemed strangely, wonderfully silent. This was one evening he wouldn't have to spend in his sanctum to get away from the sound of the radio.

He didn't even want to drink, especially, although he poured himself a glass of wine to sip. He sat at the kitchen table because the kitchen seemed more comfortable, more homey than either the living room or the bedroom. He sighed and relaxed.

So his idea about the Nelson pictures had been good. Strange that no one had thought of it at the time. Understandable why the sheriff hadn't, but it seemed a bit strange that Callahan had missed that particular boat. Unless he hadn't known of the pictures. Callahan could have published pictures of the pictures in his *El Crepúsculo* and could have seen that copies went to likely places. It would have been a feather in his cap if his newspaper had helped to locate a murderer.

On sudden impulse he left his drink standing on the table, put on his coat and started to walk to Callahan's. There was a thin sliver of moon and bright stars, between them giving just enough light so he didn't have to use his flash to see the road as soon as his eyes had adjusted themselves to dimness.

He thought, it must have been just about like this the night Jenny was killed. And she ran through it just about as far as I'm going to walk. The distance to Callahan's is the same as the distance to her grave. Had Callahan lived there then? He'd have to ask.

It seemed like quite a long walk.

The lights were on at Callahan's, so he knocked. Callahan came to the door in bedroom slippers, but he looked pleased. "Come in, Weaver." He looked around. "Didn't you bring the missus? Told you to bring her over to meet my wife."

"She went to a movie tonight. I just strolled over on sudden impulse. You're not busy?"

"Hell, no. Come in."

Weaver met Mrs. Callahan. She was tall and slender, no longer young but quite distinguished in appearance, even in a cotton house dress and an apron. Her smile was pleasant but a bit reserved and her voice, when she spoke, was soft and her diction and grammar precise. Weaver sighed mentally; he'd rather hoped that Mrs. Callahan and Vi would be compatible. They were almost antithetical to one another.

After a few minutes Mrs. Callahan excused herself to do some sewing and Weaver and Callahan were left alone.

"You said you wanted to ask me something, Weaver?"

"Yes, but first—and while I think of it—did you live here eight years ago when the murder happened?"

"No, we were renting then, in Taos; it was our first year here. We bought this place four years ago. Let's see—yes, the man we bought it from was living here at that time; he'd built the place ten years before. Artist named Wayne; he's living in New York now."

"Thanks," Weaver said. "Listen, Callahan, I've got an angle on the case I'd like to talk over with you, but it'll have to be with the understanding that you don't print anything about it in your newspaper—not until the magazine article I'm going to write gets published. Otherwise, if you break it first, my idea won't be new any more."

Callahan looked at him sharply. "You're really going in for this thing, aren't you? I don't see what angle you could get now—after eight years—that would make a new story."

"But you agree not to use it until I tell you you can?"

"Oh, sure. Won't even talk about it, if you don't want me to. What is it?"

Weaver told him about the pictures and how he intended to use them.

Callahan announced solemnly that he would be treated in a unique and unpublishable manner.

Weaver asked, "The idea *is* new? Nobody thought of it at the time?"

"Nobody knew those pictures were *left* there. I mean, no newspaperman knew about it. Hell, Weaver, there were men here from the big press services, good men. If it'd been known about those pictures being left, I flatter myself I'd have thought of using them the way you're going to—and if I hadn't, one of the other boys who covered the inquest would have thought of it. Freeman never told us about it. The stupid bastard. You say there are three of them?"

Weaver nodded. "I had them framed. And one of them's mine now—I haven't decided which one." He told the editor about the deal he'd made with Doughbelly Price to keep one of the pictures in return for frames for the other two.

"So Doughbelly knew about the pictures too." Callahan swore, and then shook his head. "Well, you're right; we missed a bet. Where were the pictures?"

"In the shed back of the house."

"Well, that partly explains it. I looked through the house and they weren't there then. That was the day before the inquest and I went out with Will Freeman. I remember I asked him if there was anything out in the shed and he said he'd looked through it and there was just junk there. I'd like to see them. Say—if your wife went in to a movie she must have taken the car. Did you walk here?"

"Yes."

"Whenever you're ready to go, then, I can drop you home, save your walking back. And I can take a look at the paintings—I'd like to see them."

"Thanks," Weaver said. But suddenly he found himself wanting to be alone again. Not that he didn't like Callahan, but what the hell; this was one of the few evenings he'd be able to spend alone in the house—in the kitchen—without being driven to the shed by the sound of Vi's radio. Why hadn't he taken advantage of it?

He said, "But—would you mind if I walked home tonight and showed you the pictures some other time? I've got something to think out—that's one reason why I walked over. My question about the paintings could have waited."

"Sure," Callahan said. "Matter of fact, I'm not too crazy about going out tonight anyway. I'll take a rain check on seeing the pictures. But you're sure you don't want a lift?"

Weaver was sure.

He walked home, as soon as he could get away without being impolite about it.

Again a quarter of a mile seemed a long distance for a girl to have run through the night, even with a killer at her heels. Certainly she must have been the better runner of the two of them to have got that far. But then, out of breath at last—

The poor kid.

When he got home he stood at the kitchen door a long time, looking out into the night beyond.

Why, he wondered, hadn't he started work on the article tonight, while Vi was gone? What was he waiting for?

Why, for that matter, didn't he start now? With the shed to work in, he wouldn't have to stop when Vi got home.

He didn't want to; that was the obvious and only answer. He didn't.

Vi came home at eleven. She was a little drunk—she hadn't been when she left—and he wondered if she'd really gone to the movie. He didn't ask.

**A**lmost all of the photographs were good. The ones of Nelson's paintings showed up especially well. Of the three shots of the shallow grave under the cottonwood two were good; of those he chose the one that had been shot toward the mountains, that caught their vastness in awful contrast to the pitiful smallness of the grave. He put that one aside on the counter of the photograph shop with the three of the paintings, and then studied the three pictures he'd taken of the house itself.

Two were good. So was the third, as a photograph, but it

was spoiled as an illustration for the story because Vi showed in it. It was the shot taken from the spot where Pepe Sanchez had stood; Weaver hadn't noticed, as he'd snapped the shutter, that Vi had stepped to the window to watch him and could be seen, dimly, through it.

Well, that didn't matter. He still had to take that interior shot, the time exposure, the first time Vi left him alone during the day and at the same time he could take another from the point where the boy had stood. That would wash things up and he could return the camera. The pictures of the paintings were excellent—he'd judged the exposure exactly right—and that was the main thing.

Weaver left the negatives of the ones he'd use with the story for five-by-seven glossy enlargements and then took the set of contact prints with him to Callahan's office.

He put down the three photographs of the pictures in front of the editor. "Came out good," he said. "Thought you might like to see them. But that doesn't cancel your rain check to drop around any time and see the originals."

Callahan bent close over the prints, studying them. "I'll be damned," he said. "They look better than I thought—judging from those water colors of his I saw. Guess he worked better in oil. Are you sure Nelson painted them? Were they signed?"

"No—but hell's bells, Callahan, don't throw monkey wrenches like that. Who else *would* have painted them, if Nelson left them behind?"

Callahan grinned up at him. "Don't take it so hard. I know how you can find out for sure whether they're his or not. When Nelson first came here he made the rounds of the galleries to see if one of them would put up work for sale. So—let me think a minute."

He stared off into space over Weaver's shoulder. "There were three galleries in town then, outside of private ones. One of the three is still run by the same man, Ellsworth Grant. It's El Pueblito Gallery, out the Santa Fe road just at the edge of town.

"And Ellie Grant's got a memory like an elephant—he's built like one, too, for that matter. If he saw any of Nelson's work he'll be able to tell you whether these pictures are really his. Only if I were you I'd take the originals to show him instead of these reproductions. They tell me color is a factor in style; each artist tends to use certain combinations of color."

"Thanks, Callahan," Weaver said. "You've been a hell of a big help to me on this, down the line. If I ever do sell the story, you've got a bottle of whisky coming."

Weaver drove home quickly and put the three framed canvases in the back of the car. He remembered having seen the sign of El Pueblito Gallery and had no trouble finding it. He went in.

There was no mistaking Ellsworth Grant, from Callahan's description of him. He weighed at least three hundred pounds. Only his eyes were small; they gleamed at Weaver through thick lenses. "May I help you, sir?"

Weaver introduced himself. He said, "Mr. Grant, I've got three canvases in the back of my car. I'd like to have you look at them and tell me if you know who painted them. I'm not trying to sell them. May I bring them in?"

"No need; I'll walk out to the car with you."

When Weaver lifted the door of the luggage compartment, Ellsworth Grant looked a moment at the top picture on the pile, then lifted it and studied the second one.

"The third is like them? By the same man?"

Weaver nodded.

"Then these two are enough; I can tell you who did them. The man who committed the murder out past Seco some years ago. Let's see—Nelson, his name was, Charles Nelson. In fact, I saw these same pictures out at his place. They weren't framed then."

"You were out there?" Weaver was surprised. He'd been told consistently until now that Nelson had never had a guest at his place before Jenny, and, after the murder, the sheriff.

"Yes, a few days after he came here. He brought in several pictures—not including these—and wanted to exhibit here and I— Let's go back in the gallery. No use standing out here to talk."

Weaver followed him back into the gallery. Grant waved Weaver to a chair and then sat down himself with a sigh of relief.

Weaver asked, "Did he just offer them for exhibit, or did he try to sell them to you?"

"To exhibit for sale, of course. Except under special circumstances—very special ones—galleries don't buy pictures. If we accept an artist's work, we show his pictures and try to sell them, taking a commission on whatever sales we make. Each gallery represents a limited number of artists, and those artists agree not to exhibit in any other gallery. Locally, that is; he may have pictures in other galleries elsewhere."

"But you refused to exhibit Nelson's work?"

"Yes. I considered it, at least slightly. It seemed to me that he had something but that his work was immature. Another few years, possibly—The six or seven canvases he brought me were interesting enough to make me want to see the rest of his work before I came to decision. He invited me to come out to his house and see more; I accepted."

"He drove you out in his car?"

"No, he led the way in his car and I followed in mine. He offered to drive me out and back, but I made the excuse that I had another errand out that way and wished to have my own car. Actually—well, I didn't *think* that I was going to accept his work and it would have been embarrassing to have him drive me back after I'd turned him down."

"I see."

"And I was quite right. He turned surly after I'd given him a definite negative. Until then he had been extremely charming in his manner; he seemed quite likable at first. Perhaps—we are all susceptible to charm—that led me to consider his work more seriously than I would have otherwise. At least to give him the break of wanting to see more canvases than he had brought in to show me."

"You really think his work had no commercial value?"

"I wouldn't go quite that far. It had some merit, but it is of a type that is very difficult to sell, and that's something a gallery must take into consideration. Our space is limited. My gallery was particularly crowded that season and I represented—still represent—a goodly number of the most important local artists. I couldn't have afforded to gamble on a newcomer unless I had been very strongly impressed with his work. So despite a personal prejudice in favor of the type of painting Nelson did, I couldn't see any way clear to representing him. May I ask where you obtained these paintings?"

Weaver explained.

"Too bad I didn't know that he'd left any pictures behind him. I would have suggested circularizing art dealers elsewhere with reproductions of them on the chance—since his style is quite distinctive—that it might have led to his capture."

"That's being taken care of now, Mr. Grant. Probably too late, but at least it gives me a good lead for an article I'm writing about the crime, and reproductions of the pictures will appear with the story."

"You are a writer, then?"

"Not exactly." Weaver explained again, briefly.

There was a soft whistling sound from a room opening off the back of the gallery. Grant said, "My singing tea-kettle, Mr. Weaver, has come to a boil. I generally brew myself a cup of tea at this time of the afternoon. Would you care to join me?"

Weaver joined him and was surprised to find that the first cup of tea he'd had in years tasted good.

He asked, "Did Nelson tell you anything about himself?"

"He talked only about his work. I asked no personal questions and he volunteered no information about himself—beyond the fact that he'd just come here and that he hoped to stay indefinitely."

"Do you think he really did, at that time? That he hoped to support himself as an artist?"

"I don't really know. He'd have said, in any case, that he intended to remain here; it would be a selling point in that a gallery would much rather handle the work of a permanently resident artist than of one who was more or less transient. But whether or not he intended to remain here, he must have been quite naive if he expected to support himself as an artist. No matter what gallery backed him, he'd have been lucky to make a few hundred dollars a year. Much better artists than he fail to make a living from their work. They teach painting or have some other means of making a livelihood."

Weaver said, "Speaking of teaching reminds me. Jenny Ames told the woman with whom she rode up on the bus from Santa Fe that Nelson was teaching at one of the art schools here. Was that out of whole cloth—a complete lie Nelson had told her—or could there have been a kernel of truth in it?"

"There could have been no truth in it at all. I greatly doubt that Nelson even applied for such a job; he'd have known better than to think there was even the slightest chance of his getting it. In fact, I can say definitely that he didn't apply at either of the two art schools which were operating then. I heard Miss Evers' testimony at the inquest and I recall now that later I asked the two men who conducted the two schools whether Nelson had applied to them. He hadn't approached them, either as prospective instructor or prospective pupil. Will you have more tea?"

"Thank you."

The big man leaned across and poured more tea into Weaver's cup. "Even today," he said, "it would be impossible for a man of Nelson's qualifications—or lack of them— to become an instructor in a school. In those days, before the G. I. bill existed, it would have been even more impossible."

"Could he have intended—even hoped—to open a school of his own?"

Grant smiled. "With no reputation, not even gallery representation? He could hardly have thought of it, let alone considered it seriously."

"What was your personal impression of him, Mr. Grant? For example, did it surprise you to learn, later, that he was a murderer?"

"Well—yes. But I did have the impression that he was a sick man, mentally and physically. Which, of course, turns out to have been the case; his crime was not that of a sane man. Also his abrupt volte-face, turning from extreme charm of manner to abrupt sullen rudeness as soon as he learned that he had nothing to gain from me, convinced me that he was definitely asocial."

"You say he was sick, mentally and physically. In what way?" Without asking leading questions, Weaver wondered whether Grant would confirm Callahan's diagnoses of homosexuality and tuberculosis.

"On the physical side," Grant said, "I noticed that he coughed quite a bit; it could have been a tubercular cough, though I wouldn't be sure of that. When I say he was sick mentally, I do not refer to the obvious fact—obvious to anyone familiar with such things—that he was homosexual." The big man smiled. "Here in Taos that is considered a minor deviation. Being asocial to the degree he was is much less normal. But I had neither of these things in mind. I think he probably—and this is guesswork—had a deep *fear* psychosis."

"If he did have tuberculosis," Weaver suggested, "would fear of death be a probable cause of such a psychosis?"

"Quite possibly. I wouldn't go any farther than that on the basis of having spent possibly two hours in his company."

Weaver tried to think of a fresh angle. "This turn-off-able charm of his," he said, "would you say it would make him attractive to women, despite his homosexuality?"

"Oh, definitely, if he chose to exert it on them. And he was quite handsome, I would say. He could have been charming to any woman, even one sophisticated enough to recognize him for what he was. A naive girl—" He gestured. "And I would judge the girl who came here to marry him to be quite naive, if only from the manner of her becoming acquainted with him—through a—what do they call it? Lonely Hearts Club."

"Do you know, by the way, if Nelson approached both of the other galleries which were operating here then?"

"Yes, he did. I discussed him with Mr. Rollinson and Mr. Stein; they were in charge of the other two galleries at that time. I was quite interested, of course, after the murder. It was the first experience I'd ever had with a murderer and naturally I was interested in comparing impressions with others who had met him.

"Their experiences, and their verdicts, were quite similar to mine—except that I was the only one of the three of us who had been sufficiently interested to accompany him to his house to see more of his work. Each of the others had talked to him, and only briefly, in their galleries and had looked only at the things he had brought to them. Each, incidentally, shared my experience of having him turn suddenly rude when he had been turned down, and each commented on how charming he had been until that point."

Weaver nodded. Even aside from verification of the authorship of the paintings, he was glad he'd come to Ellsworth Grant. The picture of Charles Nelson was beginning to round out.

He asked, "Would you have any idea why he left these three canvases behind him? Are they inferior to the others you saw?"

"The two of your three that I saw, no; they are about average, perhaps. I saw some of his work that I liked better, others that I liked less. I imagine—you said that you found these in the shed back of the house?—that he may have overlooked them inadvertently. It could have happened, especially if he packed up in a hurry, because he was apparently quite a prolific painter. He had stacks of paintings at his place; I don't see how he could have got all of them, and his other possessions, into his car—and of course he had to take with him everything he wanted; he would hardly have made a shipment which could easily have been traced. It's barely possible that he left three canvases behind simply because he didn't have room for them, but I doubt it. He would have burned them—he was certainly sane enough to have thought of the possibility of his being traced through his painting style if he left samples. I'd say that they were left behind accidentally."

"One thing occurs to me," Weaver said. "Wouldn't those paintings, if it had been generally known that they'd been left behind, have been worth something to a gallery while the murder was fresh? I mean, as the work of a murderer—"

Ellsworth Grant pursed his lips. "I imagine they would have had a certain notoriety value, that they could have been sold at that time. It would depend upon the artistic integrity—if you'll pardon the phrase—of a dealer as to whether he would have handled them for that reason. I would not have sold them for that reason myself, but I fear that one of my two then competitors—and I'll not say which one—would gladly have done so, had he known the paintings were available."

Weaver said, "Somebody in your business must have known. Doughbelly Price, who was apparently the only one besides the sheriff who knew the paintings were there—and who was technically owner of them—asked someone, he tells me, whether they were valuable and was told they weren't."

"That was I, Mr. Weaver. Yes, it was shortly after the discovery of the murder. Doughbelly asked me whether Nelson's paintings were worth anything, and I told him they had negligible commercial value. But—damn it—he didn't mention that he actually *had* any of them and I thought he was asking an abstract question so I gave him an abstract answer. If he'd only happened to mention—" Grant shrugged mountainously. "No use thinking about it now. Will you have more tea, Mr. Weaver?"

Weaver thanked him but declined and left. He drove home slowly, thinking. It was too bad neither Grant nor Callahan had known, eight years ago, about those pictures. Quite possibly, then, they would have led to Nelson's apprehension. The chances were slim now.

But what the hell, he thought; he wasn't trying to find Nelson. He was trying to write a magazine article to make himself a few hundred bucks, and it was a break for him that the right people hadn't known about those pictures at the right time.

And what more did he expect to get, anyway? Why didn't he go ahead and write the article and get it over with?

He wrote it that evening and it came easily; he found that he had to refer to his notes hardly at all and that he could write almost as fast as he could type. He did a rough draft on yellow paper; tomorrow he'd retype it on white, polishing it a little and correcting any mistakes he might have made. Then as soon as he got the other two photographs taken—the interior and the retake of the shot from the point where Pepe Sanchez had stood—he'd send the whole thing to Luke Ashley. And forget it.

And then what? Well, maybe he'd try his hand again at some more water colors. And take some long walks back toward, even into, the mountains.

He turned out the light in the shed and stepped outside, into the night. Vi's radio came blaring at him from the house, clearly audible even this far away, although it hadn't bothered him while he was inside the shed with the door shut.

He went in. Vi was sitting there listening to the radio, just listening. He raised his voice to be heard over it. "Vi, I'm going to take a little walk. Won't be gone long."

"George, in the *dark*?"

"I'll take a flashlight; I'm not going far. And leave the lights on so I can't miss the house, to get back to it."

She turned away listlessly. "All right, George." She lost all further interest in him and went back to her own dream world in a radio program.

Weaver tried to close his ears to it while he found the flashlight. At the door he turned back. There was a bottle of whisky on the table beside Vi, an almost full bottle. He hadn't had a drink all day or evening and a straight shot would go good, he thought. He deserved it after the intensive work he'd put in at the typewriter; he must have spent four hours at it, ever since dinner.

"Mind if I take some of this along, Vi? Little cool out, and I might not meet any St. Bernards."

She shook her head. He found an empty half-pint bottle on the sink and filled it from the fifth, put it into his pocket.

The night was cool and clear, a dry coolness that felt good even though he was wearing only a suit coat. Faint moon again, starlight. About as much light as this, he wondered, the night Jenny ran this way? *This* way; he was walking her last quarter-mile again. He knew now that was where he'd intended to go all along, to where Jenny's grave had been, to the big cottonwood.

He turned off the flashlight and after a moment he could see clearly enough to avoid the clumps of chamiso and to find good footing as he walked. There must have been enough light for Jenny to have avoided them too as she ran this way. One stumble, near the house when the killer must have been right at her heels, and she'd never have made that quarter of a mile.

He turned around and looked back at the house, now a hundred yards behind him and shivered a little, not completely from the cold. He took the bottle from his pocket and took a swig from it. The coyotes were howling back in the hills toward which he was heading. But coyotes are more afraid of you than you are of them.

Keep walking. The rise from which he could see the big cottonwood, and he could see it again, white wraith in the darkness, far ahead. *Jenny, how could you have run this far? You were young, you were running from death—with your life before you and death behind you, but a quarter-mile—it must have been a hell of a run, girl.*

*Jenny. Jenny Ames—*

*Down the slope, up the slope, and at the cottonwood, your grave, or what had been your grave, until a prowling coyote dug a hole that found you.*

He sat down under the cottonwood and took a drink from the bottle. Pour a libation? Or how ridiculous can you get? Wasn't he being silly enough about this whole affair? He'd already done more work on it than would have earned him a few hundred dollars back in his own racket. Not to mention the money he'd spent on photography, dinner for Carlotta, framing pictures, the trip to Albuquerque—

Forget it, he told himself; go back home and forget it except to polish that story tomorrow, take the other photograph or two, and then—*forget* it.

He took another drink, sitting there beside the faint depression that had been a shallow grave.

There's nothing for you here, he told himself. Go back. Go back to Vi, to what you have. Go back to the light, to the life that you know, the life that isn't so horrible but that you can face it and continue to live.

This is death, out here in the dark. Jenny Ames is dead, eight years dead, and death is darkness; darkness is death. Go back to the light.

Go back to life and light; no matter what that light shows, it is better than death and darkness.

Is it?

He finished the half pint and then walked back, more slowly than he had come. Behind him the coyote noises and the dark. Before him, once he had topped the rise, the lights of home. Or, rather, the light of home; only the kitchen light still burned. Had Vi gone to bed already?

Vi had gone to bed, and to sleep. He could hear her snoring lightly as he opened the kitchen door.

He went in and sat down at the kitchen table. The quart bottle stood before him, still a quarter full. But he didn't kill it; he had one more drink and one only, and after a while he went to bed. The sound of Vi's snoring kept him awake a long time.

In the morning Vi was already up, getting breakfast, when he woke.

"George, you were gone an awful long time last night. I got worried about you."

Weaver grinned. "So I noticed."

"Well, I *did*. Before I went to sleep. And those coyotes out there—"

"Coyotes aren't dangerous, Vi."

"Just the same, wandering around outdoors late at night— Have you got something on your mind, George?"

"Nothing. Not a thing."

Coffee in silence. He wondered what she'd think if he told her the truth—and then he wondered what the truth really was.

He went out to the shed as soon as he'd finished breakfast and read over the story he'd written the evening before.

It wasn't good. All the facts were there but—they sounded dull. Dull and distantly in the past. There was something missing, and it was the important part of the story, although he couldn't decide just what it was. It was the part that he couldn't put into words, even to himself.

Or could he? *Jenny Ames wasn't there, in the story.* She was a name and a few facts, but not a person. And without her, the story didn't add up.

For a moment he almost tore the manuscript across, and then he remembered that last night, after writing it, he'd torn up his notes; if he didn't keep the manuscript he would no longer have all his names and dates except those he remembered offhand.

Names and dates! Actually, that's what was wrong. That had been all he'd been able to get, and there was so much more.

Maybe Luke—no, undoubtedly Luke was the better writer of the two of them, but Luke couldn't do it either. Not from the few and naked facts—and there was so much more—

He stared again at one of the three paintings which were now again hanging on the wall. *Nelson, why?*

He was pacing, then, back and forth the five steps each way the shed allowed him, wishing violently that he'd never undertaken to write up the murder. Why do people like to read about such things? Murder is a horrible word and a horrible thing; murder with a knife is abominable. Murder stories that are fictional are bad enough, but *real* murder; isn't it a perversion for people to want to read—or write—the bloody details of the real killing of a real human being?

It's as bad for you—to want to write—

But he *didn't* want to write about it; that was the whole trouble. That was what was wrong.

If it wasn't for the fact that he needed the money so badly to help pay his expenses for a wasted summer, to help preserve the small and diminishing balance that would be waiting to finance his reentry into business in the fall or winter— If it wasn't for the money he'd already invested in camera rental, films, prints, framing the pictures, the trip to Albuquerque—

Hell, why not quit now before he got in any deeper? The thing was a gamble anyway; maybe Luke couldn't sell the damned story.

But what if the printing of the pictures did find Jenny's murderer—even now, after all this time?

All right then, *do it*. But for God's sake get it over with, no matter what the form of the story you send Luke. And meanwhile, for Christ's sake, quit having to look at those paintings—

He took them down and stacked them, face to the wall, in the corner behind the cot.

Then he went out again into the bright sunshine and stood there, just outside the shed. The radio from the house was an unintelligible murmur.

He wished Vi would go into town so he could take those remaining pictures. Maybe he could talk her into going to Taos this afternoon long enough for him to take them. If all the pictures were out of the way, off his mind, if only the story was holding him up, then maybe he could make up his mind to send it to Luke as it stood, to let Luke worry about it, or sell it.

He managed to kill the rest of the morning doing nothing. He made his suggestion as soon as they'd finished a late lunch. He'd worked out a double-barreled reason for it. "Vi, why don't you drive to Taos this afternoon and see a movie? It's Saturday, so there's one playing. Do you good to get away for a change during the day."

"All right, George. But won't you come along? I hate to go alone."

"I've got a headache, Vi. That's one reason I want to get rid of you—so I can lie down in here and sleep it off; that cot out in the shed's not so comfortable as the bed. And if you were here, I'd have to ask you to keep the radio off so I could sleep, and you wouldn't like that."

"All right, George."

"You run along now, then. I'll do the dishes, the few of them there are. And listen, if you want to stay in town to eat after the show, I can fry myself an egg or something. I know you get bored out here all the time. Take the rest of the day, and the evening if you want it, to get away for a change. Here's ten bucks."

Expensive, those last two photographs—and a chance to be alone.

He took them as soon as the sound of the car had died away down the road, and he took several shots of each so there wouldn't be any possibility of a slip-up this time.

He finished off the roll of film with a few shots of scenery in different directions from the house and then got the roll out of the camera ready to take it to Taos. Too damn bad he'd had to give up the car to get rid of Vi, so he couldn't take the films in today. But maybe if he paid extra the shop would develop and dry and print the pictures while he waited or killed time in town tomorrow.

Meanwhile, the story.

He went back to the shed and sat down at the typewriter again, staring at the blank piece of paper in it.

What was the lead sentence he wanted? He got as far as two words of it: "Jenny Ames—"

The third word and the rest of the sentence wouldn't come.

He jerked the paper out of his machine and crumpled it. The crime of murder is a meaningless thing, a mere statistic, unless the victim of that murder can be presented as a human being with a background and a history. Not as a name and a vague description.

What, really, did he know of the victim of this murder of which he was trying to write? Her name. That she was young, pretty, black-haired, that she wore a green dress the night she died. That she had been in love with the man who was to kill her and that she had come to Taos to marry him.

But from where had she come? Why had no one missed her? She must have had friends if not relatives. No one is ever so utterly alone that he can have his name publicized across a continent and have no one come forward.

It must be that Jenny Ames was not her true name; it was the only answer that made sense. Perhaps she had run away from home because her parents would not consent to her marrying Nelson and she'd changed her name so they couldn't trace her so easily.

That almost made sense. Not quite. Unless she was under age—and, according to the coroner's examination of her, she had been about twenty—why should she have feared pursuit? Her parents could not have annulled a marriage. And, anyway, wouldn't they have known Nelson's name if they had refused to let Jenny marry him?

Of course, despite that angle, age *might* have been a factor. Could it be that in New Mexico a girl cannot legally marry under the age of twenty-one without the consent of her parents? It hadn't arisen in his own case; when he and Vi had been married in Santa Fe she'd been twenty-two, and besides her parents had been dead for some years; she didn't even have any relatives living that he knew of. He'd have to ask Callahan or someone what the New Mexico law was.

He found himself walking, out under the warm sun.

Damn, if only he had the car. Besides taking the films, he could ask Callahan about that law and could ask him too how good a man the coroner had been—whether there was any chance that he had misjudged the girl's age badly enough that she could have been less than eighteen.

He was under a big cottonwood tree, the big cottonwood tree. He hadn't intended to walk there; he hadn't been paying any attention to where his walk was taking him.

He stared down at the depression that had been a shallow grave.

You thought you knew her name and description, he told himself; now you're not even sure you know her name.

He sat down in the tree's shade, leaning back against its rough trunk.

*Why did you change your name, Jenny?*

Damn it, he couldn't write that article with so little knowledge, so many gaps in the few things he did know. If he forced himself to write it the words would be meaningless things gibbering out of the pages.

*Who were you, Jenny?*

He walked back to the house. His head was beginning to ache, and that was funny in a way because a headache had been the excuse he'd given for not going with Vi; circumstances were making an honest man out of him. He found aspirins on the shelf back of the kitchen sink and took two of them.

It was comparatively cool inside the house, much cooler than it was out in the wooden shed. Adobe is wonderful stuff for hot weather; it's cool by day but holds what heat it has by night when the temperature drops outside.

He tried to read for a while and couldn't get interested. Damn it, he thought; he'd counted on reading as one of the things that would help the summer pass restfully and pain-lessly. Until recently he'd always been able to enjoy read-ing. Now, always, thoughts got between his eyes and the printed page. He threw down the book angrily.

He called himself a damned fool, but that didn't help.

He went out to the shed and got his water colors and a block of paper and brought them into the house. Maybe he could paint. He tried it, doodling idly at first and then find-ing himself trying to paint the portrait of a beautiful black-haired girl.

But he wasn't that good; a portrait takes much more draftsmanship than a landscape and draftsmanship had al-ways been his weak point. A slight discrepancy in the shape of a mountain doesn't matter but a slight one in the shape of a nose or an eye makes a portrait into a caricature. And water color is a very difficult medium for portraits, in any case.

He tried several times, but each attempt was a little worse than its predecessor and after a while he gave up. But try-ing had accomplished something—in trying to visualize Jenny, he had built up in his mind a clear picture of her, even though he couldn't get that picture on paper. It proba-bly wasn't the way she really looked, of course, but did that really matter?

He tore up the pieces of paper he'd spoiled—tore them into very small bits so they couldn't possibly be jigsawed together again—and threw them into the wastebasket. He took his water colors back to the shed.

The headache was still there, although it had dulled a bit. He took two more aspirins and then got a bottle of whisky and made himself a drink, a strong one. He sat sipping it.

He thought, I'll go crazy if I can't read anymore, if I can't find anything to *do*.

After a while the drink was gone and he made himself an-other. Outside, the shadows were getting long. Pretty soon there'd be a beautiful sunset—and nuts to bothering to go outside and look at it. When you've seen one sunset you've seen them all.

If he only had the car. He could go somewhere, go anywhere and do anything. He probably should have gone to Taos with Vi, to the movie. Watching a movie doesn't take the effort of concentration that reading a book takes. Maybe he should—no, he would *not* descend to listening to the radio. He'd razzed Vi about her radio programs so long that he'd look silly, even to himself, if he started listening to radio now, even if he could find the comparatively few programs that weren't too horrible.

He poured another drink, straight this time; it was the only thing in the world he could think of to do.

When Vi got home at eleven he was drunk, asleep on the bed.

The next day was Sunday.

It was a month, to the day, from the time he'd arrived in Taos—never dreaming, before he drove in, that he might decide to stay there. This morning he wondered why he'd made that decision.

It was raining, for one thing. Not an honest hard rain but a slow dull drizzle from a gray sky, not much more than a mist really, but more unpleasant than a real rain. But the drizzle matched his mood and his mood grew worse when, shortly after lunch, Vi made the simultaneous discovery that there was no liquor in the house except a little wine, which she didn't care for, and that it was Sunday and no liquor could be purchased anywhere.

"George, *why* didn't you get some more yesterday, before you drank everything in the house last night?"

He said mildly, "Vi, you had the car. Afternoon and evening. You knew there was less than a bottle left. If you can't get by a day without it, you should have got some."

"I can, George, you know I can. You talk like I was a lush. It was *you* got drunk last night, not me. I don't drink any more than you do, not as much, and you know the doctor told you to go easy on drinking until you get well again and—"

It went on and after a while he went out to the shed. He didn't want a drink himself, although probably by evening

he would, but he wished to hell and back there was some
whisky around, just to keep Vi shut up. There wasn't a
thing he wanted to do in the shed, and it was cool and uncomfortable there, but it was away from Vi's nagging and
Vi's radio.

He lay down on the cot and tried to sleep for a while, although he knew that if he did sleep he wouldn't be able to
sleep that night and that he'd regret taking a nap now.
Damn Sundays, he thought, damn blue laws, damn a place
where there was nowhere to go, nothing to do on a Sunday. If it weren't for this shed, his sanctuary— It's just like a
little boy's playhouse, he thought, out here in the back yard
where he can get away from people and think his own
thoughts, imagine his own imaginings. But—

*What am I? What am I imagining? Why am I here, in a dull
drizzle in Taos, earning no money when I need money, when the
money I have won't last too much longer? And if I'm not well
now, I'm not going to get well; isn't this worry worse than the
pressure of business, of working? Why don't I go back to Kansas
City and get back to work so I'll have something constructive to
think about instead of living like this?*

He went to the window and stood staring out into the
grayness and watching the thin rain fall onto the arid soil
that absorbed it instantly as it struck, leaving no trace of
moisture behind it. The ground underfoot, for walking,
would be almost as dry as on a sunny day. Dry and unfer-
tile soil, like himself, wasteland, haunted by the futile
yearning of hungry coyotes.

Maybe he should go back to the house for a hat and rain-
coat and take a walk. Better than standing here brooding.
Maybe a walk to the cottonwood where Jenny's grave had
been.

But why? What was there now?

Nothing.

He went back to the house for his hat and coat and
walked through the thin rain to the big tree, and there was
nothing, no one, there, nothing but a place where a girl had
been buried once for a short time, and that girl was long
dead and why did he keep thinking and wondering about
her?

But it was dry under the tree and he sat there a while, leaning back against the big bole, staring at grayness within and without.

He was living in Santa Fe, he thought, at the time Jenny Ames came through there on her way to be killed. She came through from Albuquerque and there was a wait of at least half an hour between buses. If he had happened to be at the bus station that day he might have met her, talked to her.

He might have—but no, she was in love with the man to whom she was going, nothing that he could have said to her could have mattered. And—even if he had known then what he knew now—what could he possibly have done? Tell her that the man she was going to marry, as she thought, was going to murder her instead? She'd have thought he was crazy. And then? Get a ticket on the bus, follow her, try to protect her? She'd have called the police, of course.

Daydream. Suppose he'd gone on the bus but without speaking to her, without trying to warn her; he could have managed to sit next to her, since that seat had been the last one taken. Carlotta Evers had been the last one on the bus and he could have beaten her to it. He, instead of Carlotta Evers, could have become acquainted with Jenny on her way to Taos. She'd have introduced him to Nelson and he could have pulled Nelson aside and said, "I know your plans; you'd better change them or I'll see that you're caught and go to the chair. If you don't want that, tell Jenny it was all a mistake, her coming here and that you don't love her and can't marry her." He could have seen that she got a room in Taos. He could have—

Weaver laughed out loud at the absurdity of what he was thinking.

You don't get second chances, knowing the future. There aren't any time machines that take you back to a point in time where you can change something that has already happened. You never know the future until it's happened, and then it's the past and it's unalterable.

The drizzle had stopped. It startled him to look at his wrist watch and to see that it was almost four o'clock and that he'd been sitting here almost three hours. Vi would be furious if she'd got a lunch ready and then had tried to find him in the shed.

He walked back rapidly and went into the house by the kitchen door.

"That you, George?"

"Yes, Vi."

"Getting hungry? I was just thinking about making us something."

It was all right, then; she hadn't missed him.

"Guess I can eat something," he said. "Our breakfast was pretty late, but that was still some time ago."

She came out into the kitchen and he went on into the living room and shut off the radio; it wasn't a soap opera, just a variety show, and she probably hadn't been listening and wouldn't miss it. She didn't.

The sound of something frying in a skillet. Vi fried everything; she didn't seem to know that there were other ways of cooking things. Not that Weaver minded fried food, but he would have liked a change from it once in a while. But he'd long ago given up suggesting variety in Vi's cooking. Just as he'd given up worrying about the way she kept house, and tried not to notice. The table beside the chair she'd been sitting in was littered, the ash tray heaping, the open box of candy, magazines lying open, an empty glass— Vi must have decided that wine, after all, was better than nothing—the lipstick on the cigarette butts and the rim of the glass— Why did Vi wear lipstick when only the two of them were here alone? Certainly not for him. Certainly not because—out here miles from nowhere—someone might come. Just habit, it must be; she wore lipstick for the same reason she wore shoes and a dress. Or for the same reason he himself shaved every day—no, that was different; his face got itchy and uncomfortable if he went a day without shaving, even if he didn't intend to leave the place.

Had Jenny Ames worn lipstick? Probably—almost all women do—but not as incessantly and as thickly as Vi. Sometimes even in her sleep if she went to bed too tight to remember to take it off, and then the pillow would be smeared with red in the morning.

*Were you sloppy, Jenny? No, I don't think you were; you were young and neat and clean.*

The crumpled spread on the sofa, the mussed pillow, the calendar askew on the wall, the unswept floor. Through the open door of the bedroom one of Vi's suitcases still on the floor, still not completely unpacked; she took things from it as she needed them and she hadn't yet needed them all.

*Jenny, you wouldn't have left a suitcase—*

Weaver sat up suddenly. Why hadn't he thought of Jenny's suitcases before?

What had happened to them?

Surely they hadn't been found; it would have been mentioned at the inquest, their contents described. Callahan would have mentioned it, and there would have been clues as to who and what Jenny had been. Even though it contains no written word, the contents of any suitcase tell much about its owner.

Or could the sheriff possibly have been as stupid about Jenny's suitcases as he'd been about Nelson's pictures? Could he have found them, looked through them casually and, if he didn't find any names and addresses, fail to tell anyone that he'd found them?

Or had Nelson taken them away, in a car that was already overcrowded with his own possessions—?

"George, lunch's ready."

He sat at the table across from Vi and ate quickly, not even tasting what he ate. He wanted to get eating over with as fast as he could so he could go to Callahan's, ask Callahan—

"George, you're acting funny. Like you're all excited about something."

He managed to slow down a bit. "Guess I was pretty hungry all of a sudden, that's all. This is good—uh—ham, Vi." He'd had to sneak a quick look at his plate to see what he'd been eating.

"Glad you like it, George. You don't often say nice things about what I cook."

"Or bad things either."

"George, I was thinking. Isn't there *any* place in Taos where we could get something to drink on Sunday? And if there isn't, we're not too awfully far from the Colorado border, are we? Is everything closed in Colorado on Sundays, too?"

"I don't know about Colorado. But it's not too near; couple of hours drive, I think. And my guess is I couldn't buy anything there either. Sorry. I could use a drink myself by now."

Vi looked down at her plate. "You know, George, I'd kind of like us to—to drink together, to get a little tight tonight, like we used to once in a while. You know."

He knew. It had been a long time since they'd had even that. At least six or seven months, before his breakdown. For the several years before that the only times they'd been able to want one another—at least at the same time—had been rare occasions when they'd been drinking together at home and each of them had got a little drunk, not too much, just enough. It hadn't happened often, and when it had happened it had been a purely physical thing but perhaps better than complete continence.

Maybe, Weaver thought, it would be a good thing to let happen tonight. There is such a thing as physical need, physical pressure. It wasn't anything mental; he didn't want Vi now, or any woman, at this moment; he hadn't *felt* any need since leaving the san, but perhaps the need was there just the same. Perhaps it was at least part of his present trouble, part of the reason why he hadn't been able to concentrate on reading or painting, why his mind insisted on dwelling on morbid things instead of normal ones.

He felt a sudden tenderness for Vi—it wasn't her fault that she was what she was and that he couldn't love her; and her problems were probably as great to her as his own were to him. The fact that circumstances and children tied them together despite their incompatibility was no more her fault than his own. Less her fault, really; as the more intelligent of the two of them he should have thought to avoid that entanglement.

He said quietly, "I'll try to think of some way to get some liquor, Vi. I'll take a run in to Taos; maybe I'll find someone who can tell me where to buy a bottle."

He drank his coffee slowly, thinking. Yes, Nelson must have hidden the suitcases, or at least their contents. Was there any chance at all that he would have hidden them indoors? Hardly, but—the outdoors was so big.

He got up and wandered around, looking. He had his story ready for her question.

"What are you doing, George?"

"Thought I might find some liquor here, Vi. Got a vague recollection of having hidden a bottle from myself one night when I was here before you came. Maybe I'm wrong, but it doesn't hurt to look."

That made enough sense to let him do all the looking he wanted.

For what? Signs of floorboards having been taken up and replaced—after eight years? That was silly, and besides if there were any loose floorboards Ellis DeLong's men would have fixed them while they were working on the place. And anyway, why would Nelson have taken up floorboards to bury something indoors when there was practically an infinity of space outside?

He went outdoors.

The shed? Again, why would Nelson have taken up floorboards and nailed them down again? He stood looking around him.

He told himself, "All right, let's pretend you're a murderer. You've just killed a girl; you buried her where you killed her, a quarter-mile back that way. You come back here and you're tired, dead tired, from the long run and from digging and pushing back dirt. And you haven't got too much stamina to begin with because you've got tuberculosis. You're worn out. But you see her suitcases—or, if they're still in the back of your car, you remember them. And just in case there should be any investigation—though you don't see why there should be, unless that woman, damn her, whom Jenny talked to on the bus should start asking questions—well, anyway you'd better get rid of them. You couldn't explain having two suitcases full of a woman's clothes and possessions. You'd better bury them like you buried the girl. But where?"

He looked around him. Sandy soil and chamiso. Distant

clumps of cottonwood, but so very distant. So far to carry two suitcases when you're worn out already.

Where, then? Weaver closed his eyes and thought. It would have been night. And Nelson would need a light to dig a hole—or at least it would be easier if he could use a light. But the light shouldn't be visible from the road—and how about that little hillock a hundred yards to the east? To go behind it would take him far enough from the house and it was the nearest place that would be completely hidden from the road. Besides, it was a spot on the way to no-where; nobody would be likely to walk there and notice that a hole had been dug and filled in. It was much nearer than the cottonwood where he'd buried Jenny, and just as safe.

The sky was grayer now and the shadows were getting long with the approach of evening, but there was still enough light for him to look there now, at least a quick look that could be supplemented by a more thorough search to-morrow. He walked around behind the hillock.

He was still in sight of the house, even though he was out of sight of the road. Vi might wonder what he was doing there—but no, he couldn't see her at any of the windows. She'd probably gone back to her chair and wouldn't notice.

A depression, that was what he was looking for. A little bigger than a suitcase, maybe three by four feet, a shallow depression. It would have been leveled off at first, maybe even a slight mound like a fresh grave, but it would have sunk in when the suitcases had collapsed later.

A small, slightly sunken area—

He picked a bigger than average clump of chamiso to use as a center and started walking in a slow spiral about it. He passed it once before he noticed it on the next round. He stood studying it—a shallow area of depression about the right size. Oval-shaped, not rectangular as he'd thought of it—but it would have weathered to ovalness, of course. And just about the right size—

Suddenly he was on his knees in the sand, trying to dig with his fingers. But the soil, sandy though the surface was, was hard packed and he stopped quickly and stood up, looking at the house.

No, Vi still wasn't at any of the windows and probably hadn't noticed him as yet. But digging would require a shovel or a trowel—or at the very least, a strong knife—and he couldn't possibly do it now without Vi's noticing him eventually. It would have to be tonight, with a flashlight, after Vi was asleep.

He was trembling a little with excitement.

He walked back to the house and went in, putting his hands in his pockets so their shaking wouldn't show. Was there, he wondered, any excuse he could use to get Vi to go into town now so he wouldn't have to wait those long hours until night? A movie? No, not after what she'd suggested.

"George, that whisky—if you're going to try to get some—"

Suddenly he realized how badly he himself wanted a drink. He said, "Sure, Vi. I'll go right away. Come to think of it, I'll try a near neighbor of ours first; I know him slightly. He just might have an extra bottle on hand, or be able to tell me where I can get one."

He went out into the gathering twilight and started the car.

**F**rom the front, Callahan's house looked dark, but Weaver left his car on the road and walked back toward it anyway. A collie came running at him, barking, and he stood still until he'd made friends with it by talking to it and letting it sniff his hand. No one came to investigate the barking and he was pretty sure no one was home, but he went on to the house anyway and knocked, waited a while and then knocked again.

He swore to himself. Callahan had been his best bet; if he hadn't any liquor on hand himself surely he knew the ropes well enough to know where some could be obtained.

He went back to the car and sat there thinking, trying to decide the next best bet. Sanchez might be able to get him some from whoever ran the tavern in Arroyo Seco, but because of the prejudice against Anglos in that town, he hated to ask any favors. Even if he gave Sanchez money and offered to pay double for the whisky besides— But damn it, besides Callahan, he still knew only a few people, all of them much too casually for him to seek them out on a matter like this. Although if he met one of them on the street he could ask casually. Perhaps that was his only chance, to drive to Taos and park, then wander around the plaza hoping to see someone he knew, however slightly. Or perhaps the desk clerk at the hotel where he'd stayed a few nights would advise him.

He had gone back to his car and was just starting the engine when a car came into sight around the next curve heading toward him—and it was Callahan's car. Callahan was alone in it; he waved and motioned as he turned in the drive toward his house, and Weaver walked back toward him.

"Hi," Callahan said. "Glad I didn't miss you. Just took the wife to a hen party and have to pick her up later. Come on in."

Weaver followed Callahan into the house. He remembered the purpose for which Vi had suggested the whisky and knew he'd better have a story ready that would enable him not to ask Callahan home with him. Vi wouldn't like that.

"Drink?" Callahan was asking him.

"Sure, thanks. In fact, that's what I came to ask you about—whether, by any chance, you happened to have a bottle or two to spare. We're caught short—friends of ours are going to drop in on us, driving through on their way from Kansas City, and they should get here about any minute now. I just realized it was Sunday and that I didn't know where to get any."

"Sure, I can spare a couple of bottles—nothing fancy, though, just drinkin' whisky. I brought back a case from Colorado a week or so ago; always bring back some when I drive up there—the state tax is enough lower to make it worth the trouble. That's a tip, in case you ever go up that way. Pick up a few cartons of cigarettes, too; you save even more on them. But you'll have time for a drink with me here, won't you?"

Weaver said he would. Callahan poured drinks for them from an opened bottle and got two unopened ones from a closet.

They sat at the kitchen table to drink. Weaver had decided there wasn't any real hurry now that his liquor problem had been solved, but he looked at his watch and pretended to decide that he could spare a little time but not too much of it. Callahan wouldn't take money for the two bottles. "Don't remember offhand exactly what they cost. Replace them any time—same brand or an equivalent one; I'm not fussy."

"Okay, and thanks to hell and back. This pulls me out of a jam." He took a drink of the whisky-and-water Callahan had mixed for him. "By the way, Callahan, how old does a girl have to be to get married in New Mexico without her parents' consent?"

"Eighteen. Why? Thinking of taking unto yourself another wife? Would your present one let you?"

"One is plenty, thanks. No, I was thinking about Jenny Ames. I've got a hunch she must have come here under a false name—that would account for nobody's having claimed her—but if she did there must have been a reason for it. It occurred to me that she could have been running away from her parents to marry this Nelson. And she could have figured that, if she was under age, they could have had the marriage annulled if they traced her. At least that's one reason why she might have used a false name."

"I don't think so. That idea was thought of at the time—by me, in fact. I asked Doc Gomez, the coroner, whether he was sure she was past eighteen. He said he'd give a hundred to one on it—that if his guess of twenty was wrong he probably erred the other way; she might have been a year or two older but not younger, certainly not two years younger."

"That's that, then. It seemed like a possibility."

"How's the story coming? Actually writing on it yet?"

"Tried one version but I don't like it. No hurry anyway; got some pictures to go with it that I haven't even taken to the photograph shop yet. And I can't send in the story till I take them and get them back."

He tried to look and sound casual. God, if only he didn't have to wait so many hours before he could get Jenny's suitcases! But there were those hours to be faced in any case, whether he spent them all with Vi or a few more minutes with Callahan. So why was he so fidgety about sitting here?

Callahan was saying, "Better not sit on the story *too* long, though. You may find our sheriff—the present one—breathing down your neck."

"Why? Where does he come in? You didn't tell him about those pictures of Nelson's, did you?"

"Nope, promised you I wouldn't, didn't I? But you forgot to swear Ellie Grant to secrecy when you showed them to him. Ellie tells everybody everything—maybe I should have thought to warn you about that, but I didn't. Anyway, he told Tom—that's the present sheriff, Tom Grayson—about the pictures and Tom likes your idea of trying to locate Nelson through them. He likes it so well he's tempted to beat you to the punch and circularize likely areas with reproductions of those pictures and a description of Nelson. Be quite a feather in his cap if he caught Nelson, after his predecessor had missed the boat. But luckily for you he came around to talk to me after Ellie had spilled the beans to him, and I talked him out of going ahead on his own—right away, anyway—at a slight price."

Weaver frowned.

Callahan waved a hand. "Oh, I don't mean money. I just mean you're to give him a build-up in your story—as being currently interested in the case whether publication of the pictures in a magazine brings results or not. Give him as much build-up and credit as you reasonably can. That way, win or lose, he'll get publicity on the deal. That magazine should sell like hot cakes in Taos, because of the local story in it. I've been meaning to look you up to tell you to talk to Tom before you sent in the story."

"I'll do that," Weaver said. "And thanks for stalling him off from trying anything on his own. Although, unless I gave him the pictures or photographs of them, I don't see how he could."

"You'd give him the pictures all right. He could get a writ to take them away from you as evidence in a murder case. Old as it is, that case is still open, don't forget. Well, he won't get a writ as long as you play ball with him."

"I will. I'll look him up and talk to him before I do the story."

"Have another drink?"

"Better not. Our company might show up any minute and my wife will be getting worried if I'm not back. Thanks for everything—for the liquor and for holding off the sheriff. What'd you say his name is?"

"Grayson. Tom Grayson. Nice guy, but he's got a temper—and a rough tongue if you get his temper going."

"I'll try not to. So long."

Weaver took the two bottles out to his car and turned it around toward home. It was fully dark by then, almost eight o'clock. He drove back slowly, not so much because the road was narrow and winding as because—the more he thought of it, the less of a hurry he was in to get home. But maybe he could get Vi drunk quickly if he kept giving her drinks, and at a certain stage of drinking she always got sleepy. But he'd have to watch his own drinking, pretend to drink more than he really did, so he'd be sober enough to do his digging after Vi was safely asleep.

He went into the house whistling, holding up the bottles.

"Better start catching up, Vi," he said. "I had to have a few drinks with a guy before I could talk him out of these, so I'm well ahead of you. Shall I make you a husky one?"

He did, and a weaker one for himself. And another and another. After a while he forgot to keep his own drinks weaker than hers, but that didn't matter; he could drink much more than she could and the difference in their first few drinks had more than evened up for the one he'd had with Callahan, so she'd be drunk before he would.

And she was. Luckily without going into the angry tirade that drink often inspired in her. And luckily, too, forgetting her original suggestion as to why they drink. Just incoherently drunk, then suddenly and overwhelmingly sleepy, then asleep in her chair, leaning back, her mouth open.

He'd wait a few minutes until her sleep was really sound, and then get her to bed. If she slept in the chair she might awaken and miss him. Once in the bed, she was safe for the night.

He walked on tiptoe and with exaggerated caution out into the kitchen, taking the bottle with him. He was still reasonably sober and he made himself another drink. After all, what did it matter if he was just a little drunk when he did his digging? Keep him from catching cold in the cool night.

He sipped his drink and he wasn't in any hurry now, he found. Now that the way was clear it was delicious to wait, to prolong his suspense. He felt ridiculously, dizzily happy; he was sorry and glad that there was no one with whom he could conceivably share that happiness. Deliberately he prolonged his drink, taking it in small and occasional sips, standing at the window staring out into the darkness in the direction in which he would soon be walking. Not that he could see anything; the sky was still overcast and the night utterly black.

The sound of Vi's snoring. Definitely safe now to put her to bed; she wouldn't waken no matter how clumsy he was.

He was just a trifle unsteady on his feet as he went back into the living room. Fortunately he wouldn't have to carry her; he knew from experience that he could get her to her feet and walk her into the bedroom, supporting part of her weight and doing the steering and that she'd walk automatically without awakening.

Even that way, it made him stagger. God, but she was getting hefty.

He got her on the bed, her head on the pillow. It would be smeared with lipstick in the morning, but he didn't worry about that. She was on top of the covers; he should have thought of pulling them back before he started, but it was too late now. He took off her shoes and then her stockings, and the touch of the flesh of her legs as he unfastened the garters wasn't either disgusting or enticing; it was as impersonal as the touch of the cool metal of the foot of the bed as he steadied himself.

It was too cool to leave her uncovered but he solved that

by folding the covers from his own side of the bed back over Vi. He himself could sleep on the cot in the shed—when he was ready to sleep—and there were two blankets out there. Anyway, sleep for him was too far in the future to think about.

He closed the bedroom door quietly behind him—although he could safely have slammed it—and went through the living room back into the kitchen.

A coat; it would be cold out there. The flashlight. Something to dig with. Damn, why hadn't he borrowed a shovel from Callahan? No, it would have been too difficult to explain. And if he found anything, no one was going to see it or know about it, ever. It was going to be *his* secret, and he wasn't going to blab about it, as he had about the pictures.

But what if the suitcases weren't—

He didn't dare let himself think that. They had to be there.

A knife would have to do for digging. He opened the drawer of the kitchen table and picked the biggest one he could find; a heavy kitchen knife with an eight-inch blade.

He stood for a moment staring at it. It had been there, with a few other implements, when he'd moved in. Could this have been the murder knife? The sheriff would have seen it, certainly, in his search of the place after the body had been found, but if Nelson had washed and cleaned it well, how would the sheriff have known?

Nobody could know now. But it *could* have been the knife. It had been there, and it was consistent with Pepe Sanchez's description.

To hell with thinking about that. It would serve for digging, or at least for loosening the packed ground. Something to scrape with. He found a small but heavy iron skillet under the sink; he could use it as a scoop too.

He had one more drink, a short one, straight.

It was cold outside, and black. But the flashlight cut the blackness and the whisky in him helped keep out the cold. He walked to the place where he was going to dig. The other shallow grave, but not—this one—empty.

The soil was hard to cut but the knife went in. He worked hard, fast. He found the skillet was worthless as a scoop; it was easier to loosen dirt with the knife and then scoop it up in both hands.

Less than a foot down he came to the top of the suitcase—or what was left of the top of a suitcase; it had been cheap cardboard and there was only enough of it left now to identify what it had been. From there on he worked with the care of an archeologist uncovering brittle bones. He enlarged the hole carefully, his hands shaking a little—either with nervousness or the cold or both—but gentle, very gentle.

It seemed to take him hours. And maybe it really did for after a while it became more and more difficult to see what he was doing and he realized that the batteries of the flashlight lying at the edge of the excavation had weakened and that the bulb glowed dully and then became only a glowing filament that cast no appreciable light.

He swore and stood up on aching legs, then walked back toward the beacon of the lighted kitchen window of the house. His teeth were chattering with cold and his hands were numb. His knees and his back ached.

He poured himself another drink of straight whisky, a long one, and sat at the kitchen table sipping it slowly, letting its warmth penetrate into his body. The ache in his back got worse instead of better, but after a while the coldness and the numbness of his hands went away.

He tried not to think about what he knew he was going to find. He tried not to think at all—because he knew that if he let himself think he'd find his sanity suspect because of the intensity of his anticipation. It wasn't, a part of his mind knew, that important. It wasn't important at all. What matter things you learn about a girl eight years dead? What matters it to touch, to possess, things that she owned, things that she wore?

You're drunk; blame it on that. You're drunk.

Another drink to drive out the rest of the coldness. A shorter drink, and he made himself drink it very slowly.

Then again the night. This time he went to the car first and got the other flashlight, with fresh batteries, that was in the glove compartment. And back to the shallow grave that was the grave not of Jenny but of the things that had been Jenny's, the things that his cleverness had enabled him to deduce and to find where no one else had ever found them nor ever would have.

He carefully scraped away the remaining dirt from the top of the suitcase and carefully sloped and shaped the banks of earth on all sides of it so that, when he lifted, no dirt would slide down into the hole.

He lifted with infinite care but the top of the suitcase came away, as he had feared it would. All right, he'd have to take the things out one at a time. He took off his coat and spread it on the ground beside the hole and put down on it first the top of the suitcase. Then other things, one at a time. A folded dress that came apart as he tried to lift it— but that taught him to be more careful with other things.

A rusty thing that had been an alarm clock. A moldy thing that had been a case for toilet articles. A soggy thing that had been a box of stationery and envelopes. Other dresses. Dampish little balls that had been rolled up stockings. Wisps of what had been silk or rayon slips and stepins. A bra. What had been a lace-topped nightgown. Two pairs of shoes that had been wrapped in paper that was now almost completely disintegrated. A woolen skirt that had probably once been white.

One after another he put them reverently on his spread coat beside the shallow excavation until the suitcase was empty. It was enough for one load; he wrapped the coat around its precious burden and carried it like a baby back toward the house. But not into the house. The shed would be his repository. He put them down carefully, first, on the cot. Then he cleared the table of the typewriter and the few other things that had been on it. He opened out the coat and transferred the things he had found carefully to the table top. Save everything, he thought; until it had been thoroughly examined, even the disintegrating top of the suitcase.

He lighted the oil stove so there'd be warmth and dryness in the shed; he locked the door behind him as he went back through the night to the excavation. He carried his coat back for the next load; it never occurred to him that the night was cold and that he might have worn it and brought a blanket for his carrying. He spread the coat again and carefully worked out the rest of the emptied suitcase, trying to tear it as little as possible. Two pieces came out of the sides, but the rest remained intact.

Then, disappointment. The other suitcase wasn't there and for a moment he thought there was nothing there. Then he saw that there was, but that probably nothing of it would be salvagable; the hole had been dug about two and a half feet deep and things had been thrown loose into the bottom of it, then the suitcase put on top. Obviously Nelson had decided that one of the two suitcases had been worthy of his own use and had merely dumped its contents into the bottom of the hole before he'd put the other suitcase—the cheap cardboard one—in.

Completely unprotected, what had been in the other suitcase was, for practical purposes, gone now. He saw the sole of a shoe but when he pulled it up, only a fragment of the upper adhered. There had been clothes, but they came apart at a touch; he couldn't tell their color, their material, or even what garments they had been.

But he went through it slowly, taking out everything that could be taken. The shoe and its mate, a comb, a chunk of what had once been leather and was about the size and shape of a woman's billfold but was now a solid thing—he handled it, nevertheless, with particular care on the chance that it might be steamed apart and disclose identification—a comb, a razor that was rusted solid but recognizable for what it had been. Some costume jewelry, the metal rusted or corroded, but the stones, when he rubbed them, as bright as new. The costume jewelry was all together; possibly it had been in a cardboard box but the box had ceased to exist. Buttons here and there. The rest had been cloth, and the cloth was gone.

Nothing more. He searched thoroughly, painstakingly, but there was nothing more.

You damned fool, he told himself, what more did you expect? Isn't this enough? Don't you know more of Jenny now than anyone else—except those who knew her before she came here? Don't you *have* more of Jenny Ames than anyone else?

He carried his coat, this time lighter than before, back to the shed. The warmth that the stove had spread showed him that he'd been gone a long time. And the pleasant shock of that warmth showed him how cold he'd been. But he disposed of the rest of his find carefully on the table before he put his coat back on. Again he locked the door before he went back to the excavation and began to scoop the dirt back into it.

The dirt didn't fill the hole again, of course, but that didn't matter. Vi never came this way and the odds were thousands to one against anyone else coming here either.

Flashlight—its batteries dimming now too—back in the car. The house again. Remove evidence. Wash and replace knife and skillet and the other flashlight. Mental note to buy batteries for both flashlights before night. Wash hands, brush clothes and particularly knees of trousers as well as possible. He brushed the dirt from his coat too and hung it back up.

His face, in the mirror over the kitchen sink, was blue from cold. He should have had sense enough to carry the things in something besides his coat. He looked around, wondering if he'd left any evidence of what he'd done. The floor was gritty with sand and dirt that had been brushed from his coat and his trousers; he took a broom and swept it out into the night through the kitchen door.

He looked at his watch and saw that it was three o'clock.

But he wasn't going to bed, at least not for a long time yet. He poured himself another drink, almost half a tumbler of straight whisky this time, and sipping at it warmed and steadied him.

The sound of Vi's snoring from the bedroom showed him that she hadn't awakened, but he went to the door and opened it, looking to be sure that she was still under the covers he'd folded over her from his own side of the bed.

This time he turned the light off as he left the kitchen; he wouldn't be coming back to the house tonight. He'd left the shed light on so he could see his way back there; he carried the bottle and a glass with him.

He sat at the table and poured himself a drink—but with extreme care so that not a drop might spill on the precious objects so near the glass. He put the bottle on the floor, safely out of the way.

He touched this, that, of the things that had been Jenny's. Could there be laundry tags on any of the pathetic shreds of what had been clothing? He searched carefully, reverently, but couldn't find any.

The box of toilet articles. He almost missed the monogram on it because the gilt had come off; there was merely a depression in the leatherette. J. A.

J. A. Jenny Ames. Or, if she had really changed her name, she'd changed it from a name that had the same initials. But then, he'd read somewhere, many people did that; it was natural when you picked a new name to use the same initials. Especially if one had anything that was monogrammed. Probably she'd even kept her right first name.

Jenny Andrews? Jenny Anderson? Jenny Adams?

What did a name matter?

He spread the things carefully so they'd dry in the increasing heat of the shed. The oil heater he'd bought for it had been somewhat too large for so small a place. It had been running full blast now since he'd turned it on and the place was getting to be almost like an oven—but that would dry out Jenny's things more quickly so he left it on, even though he himself was beginning to sweat a little in the heat.

Jar of what looked as though it had been cold cream, although the label was gone and the contents had dried to a gray crust inside it. What had been a tube of toothpaste, a toothbrush with wilted bristles but the yellow plastic handle as bright as though it had been bought yesterday. Nail scissors rusted shut forever. A tortoise-shell comb that was as good as new. A small jar, again with the label gone, possibly it had been deodorant; again only a gray crust left of what had been its contents. A little tin box that had contained aspirins. Those were the contents of the box of toilet articles.

Little things, pathetic things. Are all the souvenirs of the dead so pathetic? This comb that had once gone through raven hair, this wisp of cloth, now falling apart at a touch, that had once been silk or rayon step-ins about soft young hips. These rotting stockings that had once encased slender legs to tender thighs. This bra that had cupped rounded breasts. This frock that had hidden Jenny from a hostile world—how hostile she had never known until that final, awful hour.

Spread them carefully in the arid heat. Touch them gently with your sweating fingers, for they have not long to last and when they are gone all of Jenny will be gone; they're all that's left of her now.

He picked up the sodden box of stationery that, aside from the thing that might have been a wallet, was the highest hope. *Did you save letters, Jenny?*

No, the wallet first. He picked it up and studied it carefully. It wasn't in as bad condition as he'd thought at first, now that it had dried a bit he could open it. It stuck together and he had to peel carefully, but it came apart, and it was empty. No money, no cards, nothing behind the cellophane window except leather. He worked with it, looking for something in some compartment, but there was nothing. Either it had been a new wallet that Jenny had not yet started to use, or Nelson had carefully seen that it was emptied before he'd buried the suitcase that had contained it.

He put it down in disappointment and again pulled the box of stationery toward him across the table.

*Did you save letters, Jenny? Or, if you did, did your murderer take them out of this box as he may have taken identification out of your billfold?*

Craighill Bond; he could read the letters in the embossing on the lid of the box, although the ink of the printing was gone. He slid the box closer to him and this time the bottom of it stuck to the table and the rest slid toward him. Well, he'd study the bottom of it later. He lifted carefully and the lid came up; two sides came with it and the other two fell away.

Two piles of envelopes, stuck together in two solid pulpy masses. The paper underneath, a solid sheaf. This had been in the center of the suitcase, he remembered, or there'd be even less of it left.

One by one he peeled the envelopes apart to make certain that they were all new, unused ones—although from the uniformity of the stacks he felt sure of that already.

The paper too—until he picked up the solid sheaf of it and turned it over. The bottom sheet, although stuck to the others, was a different kind, a very slightly different size and shade, and it was written upon, although the ink of the writing was gone and there were only scratches and grooves to indicate that there had been writing there.

Weaver's hands shook and the palms and backs of them were wet with sweat. He put the sheaf of stuck-together paper down before him on the table, bottom up, and studied the scratch marks. They were clear and definite; whoever had done that writing had used a stub pen and a heavy touch; it looked like a man's writing rather than a woman's.

The final word looked like a signature. It *was* a signature. He made it out.

*"Charles."*

And the line above it. He bent and caught a reflection of the light in the faint markings. Last word of the line, *"love."* Something *"all my love." "With all my love."*

A letter—and legible—from Nelson to Jenny. And, if he'd gone through the suitcase before he'd buried it, he'd missed this letter because it had been under blank stationery at the bottom of the stationery box!

Weaver stopped a minute. He had to. He poured himself another short drink—although just at that moment he felt soberer than he'd ever felt in his life—and he poured it only after shoving his chair back from the table and being sure that neither glass nor bottle came anywhere near the precious thing he'd just discovered.

Just a short drink; he downed it at a gulp. He sat there a full minute before he pulled his chair back to the table.

How gentle can you be? That's how gentle he was as he picked up the sheaf of paper again and tried from one corner to see whether the bottom piece—the letter—would peel away from the rest without sticking or coming apart.

It would. It did. A fraction of an inch at a time—but his fingers had suddenly become precision instruments that gauged the strain to a thousandth of an ounce. It peeled away and there was writing and even the ink, enough of it to show faintly, was still there.

*"Beloved Jenny—"*

He could read that much at a glance. No date, no return address. But—"*Beloved Jenny*—"

Infinite care in a little room. A millimeter at a time he peeled, and he kept himself from trying to read more until he had the whole piece loose from the sheaf. And then the sheet was loose, separate. He put it down flat on the table.

Parts of it were more difficult to read than others, but the strokes of the coarse stub pen helped in places where the ink was faint.

*Beloved Jenny—*

*I can hardly believe that you will be with me so soon now, that all of life and happiness lies before us, then and forever, that you will be my wife for all time to come.*

*Let me know the day, Jenny darling, as soon as you can name it. I only wish that I could come to get you—but you know why it is far wiser that you come here to join me and that you leave*

End of first page.

Still no lead as to where Jenny had come from. Would there be, on one of the two inside pages?

Should he wait till he was sober before he tried to peel it apart? Until the paper was completely dry? No, maybe it would stick worse then; maybe it would stick together completely and irrevocably.

It peeled almost easily. It lay open before him.

*no traces behind you. Beloved, it is a wonderful thing that you are doing, no matter what others might think, and don't worry about the others. We'll make it all right as soon as we can, and it doesn't look as though that should take too long. We'll set the world on fire, Jenny darling; with you to help me I can do anything.*

*You'll love the place we'll live in, and you'll love Taos. It's as different from Barton as Heaven is from Hell. We'll be happier than either of us ever dreamed of being. And I'll be successful. I know the sacrifice you're making for our happiness, and I'll see that it's not in vain.*

*You'll love it here, Jenny. And I'll love you anywhere, anywhere and for ever—my bride, my love, my life, my own.*

Barton! He had the key; it could only be the name of the town Jenny came from! But where was Barton?

Let it ride till you've read the rest of the letter. Only a few words on the last page. Only pen scratchings here, but there are only a few of them.

*So hurry, darling. Make the day as soon as you can, and let me know so I'll have the license ready, and a room for you if we can't be married the first day.*

That was all, except the ending which he'd read first. *"With all my love, Charles."*

Barton! That was the important word. Where was Barton? He hurried back to the house and looked in the gazetteer section of the dictionary, but it wasn't listed. All towns of over ten thousand population *were* listed, so Barton was smaller than that. All the better; the smaller the town the easier it would be to get the information he wanted.

But damn, oh, damn it, he'd have to wait till he could go to Taos in the morning and have access to a big gazetteer to find out where it was.

But he wanted to leave *now.*

Could he wake Callahan—he'd seen quite a library of books in the editor's place and surely there'd be a gazetteer among them—at three-thirty in the morning?

Yes, he could do just that if he was willing to tell Callahan of his tremendously important discovery. But he wasn't. Besides, if he did know, at this moment, where Barton was, he couldn't just walk out on Vi. He'd have to plot and plan and lie in order to get there at all.

He'd left the whisky back in the shed and he closed up the house again and turned out the lights before he went back there for his next drink.

When he drank it he was drunk, suddenly drunk. Not mentally—his mind was as clear as the cold mountain water that flowed in the stream between his house and the road. Or so he thought. But the walls of the shed were swaying. He was pacing back and forth the length of it and he had to put his hand against a wall to brace himself at almost every turn. And the place was hot as hell by now and sweat was running down him.

How could he go to Barton? What story could he tell Vi?

His mind wanted to keep on working at it but his body rebelled; his body ached with weariness. He compromised with his body by letting it lie down on the cot. He could think lying down as well as . . .

**K**nocking on the door awakened him. Bright daylight came through the translucent window drapes and made the ceiling light, still burning, a pale yellow. The room was terrifically hot and he was soaked with sweat.

Knocking, louder. Vi's voice. "George! Are you there? Are you all right?"

He swung his feet from the cot to the floor. His shoes were still on and they hurt his feet. He shook his head to clear it and found that it ached badly and that shaking it made him dizzy. But he had to answer, and quickly.

His voice cracked when he first tried to use it, but it worked on the second try. "Yes, Vi. I'm all right. Be in the house in a minute. Make some coffee, huh?"

"Okay, George." He couldn't hear her footsteps but a moment later he heard the slam of the kitchen screen door of the house.

God, but it was hot. He could hardly approach the oil stove to turn it off; it had been running, turned to its highest heat, for—he looked at his watch and saw that it was ten o'clock—for eight or nine hours now. He used his handkerchief to turn it off so he wouldn't burn his hand. He didn't want to unlock the door and open it right away lest Vi come back for some reason and see the things that were still on the table, but he threw open the window to let some of the heat out.

He wanted to get out of the heat himself, out into the relative coolness of the bright sunshine outdoors, but first he'd have to hide the things on the table. There was a folded piece of canvas in one corner of the shed—why hadn't he used that last night instead of carrying things in his coat?—and it turned out to be big enough to wrap all of his booty. He slid the bundle back under the cot; the blanket hanging over the edge concealed it perfectly. He unlocked the door and went out, locking it again from the outside and stuffing the key in his pocket.

He felt like hell. He was wringing wet and the inside of his mouth felt like the Gobi Desert. He staggered a little on his way to the house, but once through the kitchen door he made himself walk straight. Straight to the bucket of drinking water beside the sink. He drank two full dippers of it before he went to the kitchen table and sat down.

"George, are you sick? You look—" Vi stared at him.

"Just hung over, Vi. 'Fraid I really hung one on—it sneaked up on me. You passed out early."

"But what did you *do?* Your clothes—they're *awful.*"

"Slept in them. And I guess I fell once or twice. I was out in the shed part of the time and in here part of the time. Must have fallen in between."

"But what did you *do?*"

"I told you. Got drunk. And I feel awful, Vi; lay off me, please. How's about some coffee? A cup of that and I may feel human enough to clean myself up."

"It's right in front of you, George." It was. He started to drink it.

Things were coming back to him. Barton. He had to get to Taos to find out where Barton was. But he couldn't go in looking like this. Or could he? He remembered a barbershop that had a "Baths" sign. And he wanted and needed a long hot bath, not just a sponge bath like he'd have to take here.

"Vi, I'm going in to Taos. I'll sneak in the back way so nobody will see me. I'll take some clean clothes with me and take a bath there and change—and I'll leave this suit to be cleaned. I'm such a mess that's the only way I'll straighten out."

"All right, George. But don't you want something to eat? Some eggs, maybe?"

The thought of eating sickened him and he shook his

head. "Go ahead and eat if you want to, Vi. Maybe after I'm cleaned up I'll have a bite of breakfast in town. Anything you want me to bring back?"

"Well, you can take the grocery list."

He finished his coffee and made a bundle of fresh clothes to take with him. He was still a little uncertain on his feet, he found, so he drove carefully and much more slowly than usual. His head contained a dull steady throbbing now and he had to keep blinking his eyes to keep them in focus on the road.

He parked back of the plaza and walked through an alley to the barbershop. The bath should have felt wonderful, but it didn't; his head hurt too much. And he was in a hurry because he had to get to the Harwood Library before it closed from twelve until two o'clock in the afternoon. But there was time after his bath to get a shave in the barbershop and to take his suit to the cleaners. He'd made a bundle of his dirty linen and he threw it into the back of his car and drove the few blocks to the library.

He felt a little better, not much.

He knew where the big atlas was; he'd happened to notice it on a previous stop there. He took it back to one of the tables and looked under Barton in the general index of towns in the United States.

There were two Bartons. One in Wyoming and one in California.

The Wyoming one was out, if Jenny had come directly from there to Taos, as the letter had indicated. From Wyoming she'd have come into Taos from the north, through Denver. There wasn't any way at all that she could have come through Albuquerque, a hundred and thirty miles to the south, if she'd started from any point in Wyoming.

Barton, Calif. Kern Co. Pop. 3500.

He found the map of California and found Kern County. He found the dot that was Barton and it was in the southern part of the state, about twenty-five miles south of Bakersfield. Less than a hundred miles north and slightly west of Los Angeles.

That was it, that had to be it. From there she would definitely have come through Albuquerque and on the bus which had pulled in minutes before the time she'd checked into the hotel.

He looked at the map again. How far from here? He turned to a bigger map of the Southwest that included New Mexico and Arizona as well as southern California. About a thousand miles. A day and a half to drive, if he really pushed, but he'd better figure two days each way. Four days round trip, minimum. But maybe it'd take a little digging—not the kind of digging he'd done last night—to get what he wanted. Have to allow five days, possibly six.

What story could he possibly tell Vi to account for his being gone five or six days? And it wouldn't be fair to her to leave her alone that long, way out there in the house at the end of nowhere. Besides, he'd be taking the car; he couldn't leave her there.

Well, there was Santa Fe. She'd wanted to spend some time there. She had friends; she'd kept up a desultory correspondence with at least two people there and had been wanting to see them again. Sure, he could leave her in Santa Fe and she'd be happier there than she was at the moment here. If her friends didn't offer to put her up, she could stay at a hotel.

But the story, the excuse—what on earth could he tell her that would explain his own trip and make sense?

He was still sitting there at the table with his finger on the map of California when the librarian came over and told him she was sorry but that it was noon and they were closing until two o'clock.

He apologized and said that he'd already found what he wanted; he put the atlas back on the shelf and left.

His eyes and his head bothered him again on the way home. He was glad when the drive was over and the car parked beside the house. He had to sit down as soon as he was inside.

"Did you leave the groceries in the car, George? Or did you forget them?"

He dropped his head into his hands. "Oh Lord, Vi, I forgot them. I'll go in again, at least as far as Seco, but let me rest awhile first. I've got the grandfather of all headaches."

"George, you look and act like you're really sick. Maybe

you caught a cold falling around last night. Did you lay there after you fell?"

"You mean did I lie there. I—maybe I did, Vi, but not very long. I'll be all right. Just let me alone. I want to lie down awhile."

"All right, and I'll drive in to Seco and get what groceries we really need today. Don't worry about them."

"Thanks, Vi." He went into the bedroom. Vi still hadn't made the bed but he straightened out the covers and lay down on top of them.

Vi followed him in and held a hand against his forehead. The hand felt very cool and he knew that meant that his forehead was hot. She said, "George, you've got a fever. Hadn't I better get you a doctor? You might be coming down with pneumonia or something."

"I'll be all right. Just let me alone."

"Did you eat anything in town?"

"I don't want to eat. Vi, this is just hangover; I'll be all right tonight if I can get some sleep."

"All right, George."

He heard her getting ready to go and then heard the sound of the car driving off. Groaning, he pulled his shoes back on and got up. He had to check up on a few things while he had the chance. He'd been in a hell of a shape— and a hell of a hurry, too—when he'd left the shed this morning. Had he left any evidence of what he'd been doing?

He went out to the shed and it seemed to be all right. The temperature was back to normal so he closed the window. The whisky bottle—still with a few ounces of whisky in it— was on the floor beside the table. The glass lay near it, broken. He didn't remember having broken the glass. He picked up the shards and put them into the wastebasket.

The canvas bundle, that was the main thing. Was there any chance at all of Vi's coming out here and finding it under the bed? He didn't know *why* it was so important that Vi—or anybody else—should never find that bundle or see its contents, but it was important, vitally important. Was there a better place to hide it than under the cot? He couldn't keep the door locked all the time; the mere fact that he did so might make Vi curious enough to search. And even aside from that, she might decide to change the blankets on the cot and— There must be a better place.

He found it, finally—against the wall behind the three framed canvases of Nelson. Tilted just a little more they made room for the bundle, and Vi would never look there unless she was making a deliberate search of the place.

He went back to the house, taking the bottle of whisky with him. Maybe a drink of it, straight, would help. He poured himself a medium-sized shot in a glass and made himself down it. It tasted horrible and almost made him retch but it stayed down and in a few minutes he really did feel a little better.

He took his shoes off again and lay back down on the bed. He hadn't yet gone to sleep when he heard the car coming back. Its door slammed and Vi came in. She tiptoed into the bedroom and was reaching out to touch his forehead again when he spoke to her.

"Oh, you're still awake, George? Feeling any better?"

"A little, I guess."

"Are you *sure* you don't want a doctor?"

"I'm sure, Vi. Unless I'm not all right by tomorrow. I had a spot of dog hair while you were gone and I think it helped."

She left him alone and after a while he dozed off. When he woke it was twilight outside and he felt better and he was hungry. He wasn't going to be sick after all—and that was almost a miracle after the silly things he'd done the night before, staying outdoors so long in the cold without his coat and then sleeping in a place that was like an oven and waking drenched with sweat.

Vi was cooking supper; she'd taken the radio into the kitchen with her but she'd had it going softly; he hadn't even heard it in the bedroom with the door closed.

"Feel any better, George?"

"Feeling wonderful." That was exaggerating a little but not much. He knew now that he'd be all right by tomorrow. And—maybe in his sleep—he'd figured out the approach he was going to use on Vi concerning the trip.

He waited until they were drinking coffee at the end of

the meal. "Vi, I've been thinking. You'd probably like to see those friends of yours in Santa Fe while you're out here. Be a shame for you to get within seventy miles of them and then go back without seeing them at all."

"I *would* like to see Mabel and the Colbys, George. Maybe we could go down there for a while next week?"

"Why not sooner? What's wrong with tomorrow? But listen, here's the deal; I want to see Luke Ashley, out in Los Angeles. Why can't I leave you in Santa Fe and—"

"*Los Angeles?* Why, that's thousands of miles, George. It'd take you a week, just the driving. And it'd cost—"

"Nothing but the gas. And it's one thousand miles and I can do it in two days each way, easily. I wouldn't want to stay there more than a day, maybe two at the most, just long enough to see Luke and to rest up before I start back. He'd put me up the night or two I'd be there. Now listen, and don't make objections till I finish. We both need a change—and you want to spend some time in Santa Fe and I don't. So you take your change in the form of Santa Fe and I'll take the trip to see Luke. You can stay at a hotel there unless your friends ask you to stay with them, and I'll drop you off there on my way west and pick you up on my way back."

"I *do* want to go to Santa Fe, George, but—why do you want to see Luke so bad? You did see him on his way through here, you told me."

"It's not that I'm crazy about seeing Luke; that isn't it at all. What I really want is a long drive alone, and going to see Luke just gives me a place to head for. You know, Vi, I felt better on the way out here than I have any time since. The way I really should have spent this summer was traveling—but of course that would have cost more than we can afford. But if I take one run out to L. A. and back, right now, to break up the middle of the summer, I'll feel a hell of a lot better when I get back. And we can kill two birds with one stone by letting you have the time in Santa Fe while I'm gone."

"Gee, George—"

It was as easy as that.

The details took some compromising. Weaver wanted to

leave early the next morning; he'd have started then and there if he'd dared suggest it. Vi wanted to wait at least another day so she'd have time to get clothes ready, and she wanted Weaver to spend at least a day or two with her in Santa Fe before he went on. They compromised on driving down to Santa Fe the next afternoon, Weaver to spend one evening and night there—she couldn't see why he didn't want to see their old friends at *all*—and he would drive on from Santa Fe early the following morning.

In bed that night, after Vi was asleep, Weaver tried not to think what a hole in his diminishing bank balance that trip was going to make; he'd have to give Vi at least fifty dollars for expenses in Santa Fe—although, if she didn't have to stay at a hotel, she ought to have some left out of it. His own expenses, counting gas, would probably run almost that much no matter how careful he was.

Well, if he sold the article about the murder—

But there was a catch to that. He wasn't ever going to write that article, he knew now. And neither was Luke—at least not with any data Weaver would ever give him.

He wondered how long, now, he'd known—and never quite admitted to himself—that that article would never be written. At least since last night when he'd found the suitcase. Maybe long before that.

**S**anta Fe to Albuquerque in the early dawn. Socorro, then the marker that said Arizona, New Mexico. Springerville, Globe. Three hundred miles and it was barely after noon. Ninety more miles to Phoenix. He rested an hour in Phoenix. He pushed on.

(Wonder what Vi would think if she knew he wasn't going to Los Angeles at all, that he was going a thousand miles for a rendezvous with a girl who'd been dead for eight years?)

A hundred and seventy more miles to Blythe on the

California border. And it was dark by then and he was utterly weary; he checked in at a hotel that didn't look expensive, but charged him five dollars just the same, and slept solidly and dreamlessly for ten hours.

(Vi would think he was insane. And would she be too wrong?)

He drove out of Blythe at seven, and it was a relatively short lap from there. Indio, San Bernardino.

Barton. Pop. 3500.

It was still early afternoon and he wasn't tired; the bulk of his driving had been done the day before and he'd had a good night's sleep.

(Here he was. But why was he here?)

A wide main street, the only important street in the little town. Wider for one block in the middle of town, where all the business places were. Angle parking. He parked and got out of the car.

He went into the corner drugstore first. The phone book was a ridiculous off-chance, but he tried it. No Ames listed. He had a coke and asked the proprietor if there was anyone in town by the name of Ames.

"No, sir. Don't know anyone named Ames who ever lived here. Not offhand."

"You've been here long?" Weaver asked.

"Born here, fifty years ago."

"And lived here all that time?"

"Except a few years during the war. The *first* war, I mean."

Weaver drank his coke and didn't ask any more questions. There were other questions to ask, but not in a place where he had already mentioned the name Ames.

He had a sandwich and coffee at the restaurant three doors down. The waitress didn't look like a good bet. Too young; eight years ago she'd have been in the third or fourth grade of school. But it didn't hurt to try.

"You lived here long, Miss?"

"All my life, except for one year, last year. I worked in L. A., but I didn't like it and came back home."

"I was wondering," Weaver said. "I used to know a girl from Barton. First name was Jenny and I can't remember her last name. I think it began with an A. Do you know who I mean?"

"Jenny? I'm afraid not, not if her last name is an A. I know a Jenny Wilson; she was in my class at high school."

"She wouldn't be the one—unless you're a lot older than you look. The Jenny I knew—she'd be close to thirty now."

"No, it wouldn't be Jenny Wilson, then. She's only nineteen, not even as old as I am. You might ask Pop; he knows about everybody that ever lived here."

"Pop?"

(Surely not Pop. 3500?)

"My father. Up by the cash register. You'll meet him when you pay your check."

Weaver finished his sandwich and coffee, left a tip and went to the register. The man behind the counter rang up forty-five cents and gave him change. "Kind of hot out today," he said.

"Sure is. By the way, I'm trying to remember someone I knew once who came from Barton, about eight years ago. Your daughter says you know about everybody who ever lived here." Weaver leaned on the counter casually.

"Well, try me. I know a lot of people."

"A girl named Jenny. I think the last name begins with an A, but I can't remember it. She'd have been around twenty when she left here."

"She was twenty-two. Jenny Albright."

Weaver reached for a cigarette in his pocket and then realized that his hands might tremble when he tried to light it, so he didn't try it.

"That's the name," he said. "Her folks still live here?"

"Her mother does. Her father died, year or so after she went away. Sure, I remember Jenny. Nice girl, although—"

"Although what?"

"Nothing. I just meant I didn't really know her very well."

"I'd rather like to talk to her mother while I'm here. Do you know where she lives?"

"A few blocks from here, on Beech Street. That's the next street north, parallel to this one. I don't know the house number but I guess it's in the phone book. What's Jenny doing now?"

Weaver said, "I don't know. I've lost track of her; I'm trying to find out where she is. Well, thanks a lot."

He went out into the hot sunlight and stood a moment indecisively. Should he look up Jenny's mother next? Or talk to a few other people first, get a few more preliminary facts to make his story better? Maybe he should do that; he could use a drink, for one thing, and bartenders are usually talkative if their customers want them to be. And he hadn't had a drink since night before last, in Santa Fe with Vi and her friends.

He found a tavern a few doors away and it was dim and cool and comfortable inside. He was the only customer and the bartender looked more than old enough to remember eight years back if he'd lived here that long.

Weaver ordered a whisky and soda. "Nice little town, Barton," he said. "First time I've ever been here but I like the looks of it."

"Yeah."

"You lived here long?"

"All my life in California. I'm a native son, born in Mojave. Lived in Barton fifteen years."

"Sure a nice little town, Weaver said again. Have a drink with me?"

"Sure, thanks."

"Used to know a girl who came from here. Jenny Albright. Remember her?"

"Henry Albright's daughter?"

"If she ever mentioned her father's first name I don't remember it. But she said he died six or seven years ago."

"Yeah. Well, I didn't really know her personally, just by sight, and I'd forgot what her first name was, but that must be the one. If it is, and if she knew her father died, it was funny she didn't come back or write or anything. I remember people wondering about it."

Weaver said, "I think she learned about it quite a while after it happened. What did Henry Albright do?"

"Head teller at the bank. His daughter worked there too, up to the time she left."

"Oh," Weaver said.

"Look, mister, are you a detective or something?" The bartender didn't sound belligerent, just curious.

"Me? Hell, no. Why?"

"Just remembering something about the way the girl left town."

"How was that? And will you make us two more drinks?"

"Sure. I dunno, maybe I shouldn't have said anything. But a lot of people wondered and there was a lot of talk."

"You mean she got in trouble?"

"Well, not the kind of trouble girls usually get in, if that's what you mean. She was a good girl, I guess, that way. From what I heard, her parents were so strict with her she *had* to be. Henry wasn't a customer here—he practically ran the local Baptist Church, and I guess he pretty much ran his family too. Hard and strict, and his wife too. I don't know as I blame any daughter of his—especially an only child— for taking her walking papers."

"If that was all she took," Weaver said. "I gather that's what you were hinting at."

"Well, that was the talk. Nobody knows for sure, unless people at the bank. And if she did take anything from the bank when she left, Henry must've made it up."

"Is there any indication that he did?"

"Well—say, you're sure you're not a detective or anything? Nobody knows, so I don't want to get the girl in trouble or keep her from getting a job or whatever it is."

"Nothing like that," Weaver said. "In fact, Jenny Albright is dead, so you can't get her into any trouble if you tried. And if her father's dead too—well, it can't make any difference. No, I knew Jenny just well enough to be curious about—well, what she was really like."

"You're not kidding me about her being dead?"

"No. Honestly."

"Well, then it doesn't matter. She left suddenly, and some people here thought she might have taken money from the bank with her. There were a couple of things that made it look that way. For one, she never wrote home again, as far as anybody knows. For another, just after she left Henry

Albright sold his home—one that he owned outright—and bought a smaller place, with only a down payment on it. Looked like he was raising money."

"Seems funny a girl would do something like that to her own family."

"Yeah, but maybe she didn't figure that her father would make it up out of his own pocket, just thought she was stealing it from the bank. And maybe she never knew that he did make it up. Say—"

"What?"

"Just wondered something. If she really did run off with money from the bank, it's funny she was using her right name when you knew her."

"She wasn't. I happened to find out her right name accidentally—and after she died."

"Oh. Well, like we were saying, it's still funny that a girl brought up like that—no matter how strict her parents were—would suddenly up and embezzle from a bank. My guess is, if she did, there was a man in it somewhere and she was doing it for him. Some women'll do anything for a man if they love him."

"I guess so," Weaver said. "It couldn't have been any of the local swains, could it? I mean, did anyone else disappear about the same time Jenny did?"

"Nope. I guess—I'm remembering more about it now—I guess maybe that was part of the trouble with her, that she never had any local dates to speak of. Her parents were hellers when it came to things like that, wouldn't let a man get within fifty feet of her, even after she was twenty. I remember hearing that a guy she'd been corresponding with came to town once to see her—dunno how she got into correspondence with him—but anyway—"

"Was he an artist?"

"I wouldn't know. Anyway, way I heard it, she got to see him a few times and then her parents learned he was around—she must've managed to keep it secret up to then—and clamped down the lid, wouldn't even let her out of the house. Nope, I don't blame her for running away. Not too much, even if she stole money to take with her. Served the old heller right, way I see it. You can't treat a girl over twenty like she was fourteen and living in a nunnery at that, not without expecting her to bust out one way or another."

Weaver nodded.

He had the picture now, probably as clear as he'd ever have it.

*So that was it, Jenny. And you were so starved for romance that you wrote to a Lonely Hearts Club and got into correspondence—you must have used a post-office box or general delivery so your mother wouldn't see the letters—with a man who sounded wonderful and romantic. And he came to see you, and he made love to you and said he wanted to marry you, so you fell head over heels in love with him.*

*Then your parents learned he was here and kept you away from him. (Why didn't you just tell them off, Jenny? It must have been because, from so many years of submission, you were afraid to or didn't realize that you could.) But back to the prison of your home, losing the man you loved, as you thought.*

*And then, again, his passionate letters. And he wanted so badly to marry you right away, but it might have to be years because he had to wait until he'd saved up enough money to start his art school in Taos. If he only had five thousand dollars, or ten, or whatever he figured your bank carried in ready cash (Had he pumped you about that, Jenny, while he was here?) he could start his school at once and marry you right away.*

*And you loved him madly—*

"Have another one, mister? On me, this time?"

"Huh?" Weaver was startled. He'd forgotten where he was and to whom he'd been talking. "Oh, sure. Thanks."

"I was just thinking. About Mrs. Albright. If you're *sure* her daughter's dead, she ought to know about it. I don't like her much—she's like her husband, Temperance and trying to get local Prohibition and close us up and stuff like that. But just the same, if you're sure Jenny's dead—"

"I'll tell her," Weaver said. "You're right; she ought to know."

"Or if you haven't got time, Mr.—"

"Weaver. George Weaver."

"Glad to know you; my name's Joe Deaver. Say, that's funny; our names rhyme. Weaver and Deaver. Anyway, I was just going to say if you haven't got time to see the old battle-ax or if you don't find her in or something, I can get word to her for you. My wife's a Baptist, too, goes to the same church. I don't go for that kind of stuff myself."

"Thanks," Weaver said. *(What was your mother like, Jenny?)* "I'll look her up, if she's home. If she isn't—well, in that case I'll drop back and let you know. Or maybe I can phone her from here and make sure she'll be home. Mind if I look in your phone book and then use your phone?"

"Help yourself, Mr. Weaver."

"Make us a couple more drinks while I do."

Mrs. Henry Albright was listed in the phone book. Seven-eighteen Beech Street. One-eight-two-R. Weaver found a nickel in his pocket and called the number. A female voice answered.

"Mrs. Albright?"

"Yes."

"You don't know me, Mrs. Albright. My name is Weaver; I'd like to see you for a few minutes, if I may. I called to be sure you'd be home."

"Yes, I'll be home all afternoon. What do you want to see me about?"

"A personal matter, Mrs. Albright, something I'd rather not explain over the phone. But I'm not selling anything, and it *is* both personal and important."

"Very well. I will be here."

He didn't like the sound of her voice; it was cold and hard.

"Thank you, Mrs. Albright. I'll be there within half an hour."

He went back to the bar. He rather wished now that he'd settled for getting word to Jenny's mother through Joe Deaver—but Joe had heard his end of the conversation and he couldn't change his mind now.

He drank his drink and decided that another would help. "Two more for us, Joe."

"Thanks, but I'll skip this one. I've got six hours yet on this shift."

"Okay, but don't skip mine. From the frost on that woman's voice, I'd better be fortified."

The bartender chuckled. "What the hell do you care? You're doing *her* a favor. But, come to think of it, you'd better stay sober or you won't get inside the door."

"Which wouldn't sadden me too much, Joe. But I'll be sober. I'm used to drinking at high altitude where drinks hit you harder. Down here near sea level, I'd have to drink twice as much as usual now before I'd start to feel it."

"Know what you mean. I was in Denver once, and that's only a mile high and I could tell the difference when it came to drinking. How high is wherever you come from?"

"Seven thousand. Taos, New Mexico. It's seventy miles north of Santa Fe."

"Is that where Jenny Albright died?"

"Yes."

"Of what?"

Weaver hesitated. He'd been talking too much. He said, "I don't know, exactly; I learned about it a long time afterwards."

"Oh. Sure hot, isn't it? Wonder why Jenny went to Taos. I had a hunch it was Tucson, Arizona."

"Tucson? Why did you think that?"

"Well—I never mentioned it to anyone because if Jenny *did* run off with money from the bank, I was for her. But it doesn't matter now. About a year after she left here I was driving east and stopped over in Tucson the first night. I saw a guy on the street there that I thought was the guy who'd come here to see Jenny. And if it was him she ran off to go to, I figured maybe she was there too. But it was none of my business; I didn't hunt for her."

Weaver saw that he'd spilled part of his drink. He put down the glass on the bar. "You're sure it was the same man?"

"I thought it was. He was wearing his hair different—longer; he had a crew cut when he was here. And he had a mustache. But I thought it was the same guy. He was in here a few times for drinks during the few days he was in Barton, so I knew him pretty well by sight—but it was afterwards that I learned he'd been here to see Jenny. You know how things get around in a small town."

"Did you speak to him? In Tucson, I mean?"

"Nope. I just passed him on the street and I wasn't *sure*. And besides, if Jenny *was* with him, married or otherwise, and she had really swiped money from the bank here—well, it would have scared them to have been spotted. So he didn't notice me and I didn't speak to him."

*Tucson.* T. b. It fitted; it had to be. He'd already guessed that Nelson had doubled back from Amarillo to get to the hot dry Southwest, and Tucson was right in the center of that. And the change in haircut, the mustache—they made it even more likely that Joe Deaver had seen the right man. It added up.

But seven years ago—

"Give me one more, Joe. Then I got to get going."

"Sure, Mr. Weaver. Wish you were sticking around Barton awhile longer, though. You're a good customer."

Weaver managed to hide his excitement and wisecrack back, to force himself not to gulp the last drink.

Then the hot sunshine again, and he'd had a bit more to drink than he'd thought. He wasn't drunk, but he wasn't completely sober either. He'd done a hell of a lot of drinking within the space of less than an hour. But what the hell—look at all he'd learned.

He started his car and he was in such a hurry to get to Tucson that he almost decided not to go to the Beech Street address to see Mrs. Albright. But—he'd promised. And what the hell difference could ten or fifteen minutes make? He found the house, he found the door, he found the knocker.

She was tall and thin and pale and gray. She had lips like rubber bands and eyes like buttons too small for their buttonholes.

"Mrs. Albright?"

"Yes, I'm Mrs. Albright."

"My name is Weaver. I just called you on the phone. I'm afraid I have bad news for you. About your—daughter." He couldn't help the hesitation on the last word; he couldn't think of this woman as ever having had a daughter, as ever having undergone the necessary preliminaries to having a daughter.

"Mr. Weaver, you have been drinking. Your breath is offensive."

"My breath is irrelevant, madam. I—" How the hell can you tell a woman who antagonizes you at sight and is antagonized by you, bad news and sound sympathetic about it? "I'm sorry, Mrs. Albright, I'm afraid I must tell you that your daughter is dead."

"When? Where?" She might have been asking a laundry-man when the laundry would be delivered—if she didn't like the laundryman.

"A few days after she left home. In New Mexico."

"And your purpose in telling me this?"

"I thought you might be interested. I see that I was wrong." He bowed slightly, not quite losing his balance. He turned and started for the porch steps.

"Mr. Weaver—" Her voice sounded almost human. He turned back. "Mr. Weaver, perhaps I owe you an explanation. I *am* sorry to learn that Jenny is dead."

"Very big of you, madam."

"But no more sorry than to learn of the death of anyone. She was not our daughter as of the time she left us. You did not know that, of course, so your reason for coming here was generous if misguided. Thank you."

"Thank *you*," Weaver said, "for being so kind as to be interested."

The door was closing. Damn the bitch. He wanted to hurt her. If he could. "I thought," he said, "it might even interest you to know the manner of her death." The door stopped closing, a few inches open. He said, "A madman killed her with a knife."

As good an exit line as any. He went back to his car and got in. He glanced back and the door had closed. But he felt sorry and ashamed of himself. He almost opened the door of his car to go back—but what could he possibly say that wouldn't make things worse than they already were? And she *had* asked for it. What the hell kind of mother had she been, not to be interested in what happened to her own daughter? If Jenny's father had been anything like her mother, how had she ever lived at home for twenty-two years—and why hadn't she taken the whole damn bank with her—some sum that her father couldn't possibly have paid back? Oh, yes, they'd paid it back, but out of pride, to save their own name and reputation, not to spare Jenny pursuit and prosecution.

He drove out of Barton fast, turning corners viciously. On the open road he upped the speed to eighty to get away from the place.

Could he make Tucson tonight? He pulled off the road and studied a map he'd picked up at a filling station the day before. Tucson was six hundred miles away and it was after three o'clock in the afternoon now; no, he couldn't possibly make it tonight. But he'd push on as far as he could before he holed in, get an early start in the morning, and try to make Tucson by noon.

San Bernardino, Indio, Blythe. And it was nine o'clock. Up at seven and off at eight. Phoenix at eleven o'clock, Tucson at half-past one.

What now? The police? No, *not* the police. Too much to explain, and everything given away, the whole thing in the newspapers. He'd have to see what he could find out by himself, and then decide what to do about it. Chance in a million, probably, that Nelson would still be here after seven years. Best he'd be likely to get would be a lead to the next place Nelson had gone.

Two lines to work on. Picture galleries—thank God he'd brought his photographs of Nelson's pictures with him on the off-chance that they'd come in handy. Sanatoriums that took t. b. patients, in case Nelson's t. b. had developed to the point of hospitalization during his stay here.

Try the sanatoriums first, he decided.

He put his car in a parking lot in the middle of town to get it off his hands; since he didn't know the town, he'd save time using a taxi.

He went to the Chamber of Commerce first; a woman there gave him a list of sanatoriums that specialized in t. b. cases and, with her help, he crossed off several that had started within the last few years. There weren't as many as he feared; he should be able to cover them in one afternoon.

Telephoning would be useless, of course. Nelson certainly wouldn't have registered under the name he'd used in Taos; in each case he'd have to find someone who'd worked there at least seven years and try to identify Nelson by description. It was going to be tough going, he thought.

It turned out to be easy going, ridiculously easy going. He hit it on the second try. A small gray-haired man with thick glasses and bright eyes looking through them sat behind a desk and said, "Yes, we had a patient of that description. Ah—I can look up the records if it's important to be exact, but offhand I'd say he came to us between six and seven years ago. He was here two years."

Weaver leaned forward, his fingers digging into his knees. "And do you know where he went when he left here? Have you been in touch with him since?"

"He died here. His tuberculosis seemed to be only pulmonary when he first came to us, but it developed into tuberculosis of the bone—of the spine. We tried surgery, spinal fusion, but it did not help. You say he was a murderer? Then his case, I fear, has long since been settled before a higher court."

"I see," Weaver said. He felt strange, somehow. "If you don't mind, doctor, I'd like to make sure, absolutely sure, that we're talking about the same man. You say he was an artist. Did he do any painting while he was here?"

"During the first few months we allowed him to paint a few hours a day. After that, he was unable to continue. But he completed several paintings during that time; one of them is on the wall behind you."

Weaver turned and looked.

Mountains, in colors and shapes such as mountains have never been. Mountains that writhed in dark agony against spectral skies, mountains of another dimension, in another world, under an alien sun. Nelson's work, beyond the remote possibility of a doubt, as individual as his fingerprints would have been. Possibly more individual; in infinity fingerprints might repeat, style never.

Weaver looked at the picture for a long time. The voice of

Dr. Grabow came over his shoulder. "Interesting technique. Not many people like it, but I do. Dealers have told me it is worthless—not that I tried to sell it; it happens that several have been here in my office on other business and I asked them out of curiosity. But I like it. There's something—"

Weaver asked, "Was he mad?"

He turned back and looked at the doctor, who was smiling. "What is madness, Mr. Weaver? I am not a psychiatrist, so I do not know. If I were a psychiatrist, I would know even less. Nothing is more confusing than trying to define madness. I don't even know whether I am sane myself. Do you?"

Weaver said, "I want to know. I really want to know. Was he insane?"

"He was a sadist, I believe. Sadism is mental abnormality—whether or not it is insanity, I do not know. The sadism was latent while he was here, but it might easily have become active, given opportunity. He was homosexual, of course—you mentioned that yourself in describing him, and you were quite right. Homosexuality again is an aberration but is not insanity, definitely not. The point at which he nearest approached true insanity—whatever that is— would be his fear psychosis. He feared death. Everyone does, of course, but in his case the degree of fear was probably psychopathic. He killed for money?"

"Yes," Weaver said. "He killed for money."

"Understandable. Desperation, the fear psychosis. If he needed money in order to give himself the treatment that might have saved his life, I do not doubt that he would have gone to any length to get the money he needed."

"How much money did he have?"

"Somewhere around ten thousand dollars, I would say. Enough to pay his way almost—not quite—to the end. Including the surgery he underwent. He wrote checks regularly until the last month or two. By then all surgery had failed and he was a dying man; we knew that he had only weeks to live and he had already paid us so much that— well, we're not a charity institution but we didn't have him transferred to one. We carried him through."

*A better break, Jenny, than he gave you. Or was his death worse than yours? He must have seen it coming—longer, much longer.*

Weaver stood up. "Thank you very much, Dr. Grabow." His voice sounded strangely flat to him. He looked again, on his way out, at the twisted mountains in the painting on the wall.

The hot sunlight. Fourteen minutes after three o'clock, and it was all over. He knew the whole story now. And there was nothing to do about it.

There's never anything to do about something that happened years ago—or yesterday or a minute ago.

He went back to his car in the parking lot and sat in it to study his road maps. Over five hundred miles back to Santa Fe. And what was in Santa Fe? Vi. No, he couldn't possibly make another five hundred miles today and tonight, not possibly. He felt let down, worn-out, dull, passive. And anyway he was still ahead of schedule; Vi wasn't expecting him before tomorrow evening or the evening after that.

Some problems multiply themselves. He had a drink and he got drunk. It got dark and he got drunker. It wasn't a happy drunk; it was a dull brooding one.

There must have been hallucinations in it because—sometime, somewhere—there was a man, a big man, who said, "Mr. Weaver?" He said, "Yeah? My name's Weaver." Not belligerently, not worriedly, not anything at all. And the big man peeled back a lapel and said, "Police. Like you to drop around to the station. They want to talk to you." And under the lapel was a badge. It was interesting. Weaver said, "Sure, pal. How'd you know my name?" And the big man said, "I asked you and you told me." And that didn't make sense, but he went with the big man and they took him to a room with bars and there was a cot in the room; he lay down on the cot and slept and then somebody shook him and said, "All right, you can go now." "Go where?" "Anywhere. Listen, mister, it's all right; we made a mistake. We're sorry. Now beat it or we'll change the charge to D and D." "D and D? What the hell is D and D?" "Drunk and disorderly. Now listen, you're drunk and you know it and I know it and if you want to sleep it off here, it's okay by us. But—we're telling you to scram if you want to scram and if you don't you're being disorderly—and that adds up to D and D and if you're smart you'll scram because there'll be a fine tomorrow if we have to book you D and D." A fine tomorrow. It was all mixed up, however the hell he tried to interpret it, but what the hell, he wasn't belligerent and he didn't want trouble with anybody so he scrammed, and afterwards he knew it hadn't really happened because it couldn't have—not with a cop picking him up by name when nobody knew his name and he was just on the way through. Yes, here he was back in a bar—the same or another—and it was a screwy dream he'd had because it couldn't have happened. It was just something that he remembered that didn't happen, and some other things must have happened that he didn't remember, because he woke up in a hotel room and had no recollection of having got there; the last thing he remembered was the man from Chicago who was explaining—what was it?—in such great detail. Anyway, he awoke in a hotel room, asleep in his clothes although he'd taken his shoes and coat and tie off, thank God. And his money—except about twelve dollars, and he must have spent that—was still in his wallet so that was all right. His watch had run down and he phoned down to the desk and learned that it was ten o'clock.

His suitcase wasn't with him; he must have left it in the car. No use taking a bath until he had clean clothes to put on afterwards, so he went downstairs, oriented himself and found the parking lot—only two blocks away, luckily—and carried his suitcase back to the hotel.

As he bathed and dressed, something puzzled him. What was that crazy memory he seemed to have about having been in jail the night before? Arrested without charge and released without explanation—and the big man who'd turned back his lapel to show a badge—had all of that been a dream? It must have been; it didn't make any sense otherwise.

He drove out of Tucson before noon. About five hundred miles to Santa Fe. Well, he could make it in ten hours if he kept going. He kept going. Not thinking—any more than he could help—just driving. Sometimes through mountains—but on wide, easy roads—sometimes across the open desert where he could make eighty without even feeling that he was going fast.

In spite of a stop to eat in Lordsburg—he didn't know whether it was breakfast or lunch or what—he made Socorro by seven o'clock—and he was tired then but it was only seventy-five miles to Albuquerque and another sixty to Santa Fe; he could make that in not much over two more hours, so he kept going, stopping only for a sandwich and coffee.

Santa Fe, nine-thirty. He stopped at the outskirts of town so he could phone the Colbys, with whom Vi was staying. He hoped she'd be there. If he could talk Vi into it, he'd push on the last seventy miles to Taos—and the ten miles beyond—tonight, to get it over with, to get back home. But there was no answer at the Colbys'.

He drank coffee to keep himself awake, realizing now that the driving was over, how utterly tired he was, and how miserable mentally and physically. He didn't even want a drink—after a binge like last night's he seldom felt able to drink again the next day. And he'd been drinking too damned much anyway.

He phoned again at ten and again at ten-thirty. They were still out. And by then he realized that he was too tired to face that last eighty miles of driving even if he did contact Vi—and that he'd rather check into a hotel and get a long night's sleep than reach her now and be talked into coming around and joining the party, whatever they were doing.

He took a room at the Montezuma and fell sound asleep the instant he got into bed. He slept eleven hours; it was ten o'clock in the morning when he awoke. He had breakfast and phoned the Colbys at eleven.

"George, old boy!" Wayne Colby's voice said. "Been hoping to hear from you. Come on around for lunch with us."

"Just had breakfast, thanks. But I'll drop around to pick up Vi. Like to get started back to Taos right away."

"Don't be silly; you're going to give us an afternoon at least. Look, today's Saturday, that's why I'm not working. And what's wrong with going back to Taos tomorrow, Sunday?"

"I—well, I'll drop around and we'll talk about it, Wayne."

He didn't have an excuse ready to explain why he couldn't stay over, but the stall would give him time to think one up.

He had one ready by the time he reached the Colbys' apartment, and he didn't push it too far; he said they had to leave Santa Fe in time to get back home by six o'clock, and that gave him several hours to spend with them. Rather boring hours and he was constantly having to say "Pardon?" when somebody asked him a question and he hadn't heard it, but the hours passed.

He pried Vi away at four o'clock. Taos at five-thirty. He'd pleaded a six o'clock appointment to the Colbys as his reason for having to leave at four, but on the way back he explained to Vi that he didn't really have one; he was just tired of traveling and of being away, that he was now in a hurry to get back home.

He wondered if he really was. And, if so, why.

"George, it's Saturday, remember. We'd better lay in some liquor, hadn't we, before we find we can't get any on Sunday?"

"Sure, Vi." He remembered the two fifths he'd borrowed from Callahan and got five bottles so he could return Callahan's two. But Callahan's place was dark when they drove past it, so he didn't stop. He'd take it over to Callahan tomorrow.

Six o'clock when they got home. Weaver parked the car while Vi unlocked the door and went in. She'd turned the kitchen light on and was standing in the middle of the room, looking around, when Weaver joined her.

"George, I think somebody's been *in* here."

"Why, Vi? Anything gone?"

"Well—not that I can see—but things have been *moved*."

"I'll—just a minute." Weaver went quickly through the rest of the house. No one was there, then, but someone had been there all right. Things on top of the dresser had been moved and the drawer in which he kept his shirts was closed all the way—he always left it an inch or so open because it stuck when closed tightly. After a struggle or two with it, he'd stopped closing it completely; he was sure he hadn't done so when he'd packed for the trip.

He joined Vi in the kitchen. "Nothing gone that I can see,

Vi." He didn't want to worry her, so he didn't mention the drawer. "Are you sure things have been moved?"

"Well—*almost* sure, George. But there's nothing gone that I can find."

He grinned. "If anything was gone you of course couldn't find it." He went to the kitchen door. "Well, I'll look around the rest of the place."

Not to be too obvious in heading quickly for the shed he walked once around the house itself and even opened the door of the outside toilet and looked in before he went to the shed.

Were there scratches on the padlock? Yes, but he couldn't be sure that they hadn't been there before without his having noticed. He went inside and turned on the light.

His portable typewriter was still there, probably the only thing in the shed that could have been stolen for resale. His eyes took that in and then went to the three stacked pictures behind which the canvas bundle was hidden. He could see canvas at the end of the pictures—and he'd hidden it carefully; it hadn't showed before.

He took out the bundle and opened it on the floor, kneeling. The shreds of clothing, the toilet articles and their case, the fragments of the suitcase and the remnants of the box of stationery. All there. All there but one thing. The letter Nelson had written to Jenny was gone.

Weaver locked the shed behind him, wondering why he bothered, and walked back to the house thoughtfully. Who in hell would have searched the house and the shed and have stolen only that letter? It didn't make sense.

Jenny dead eight years. Nelson dead four or five. Case closed.

Vi was frying eggs. He said, "Nothing missing, Vi, that I can discover. Nobody around. You must be imagining things."

"Guess so, George. Want to make us a drink before we eat?"

He made drinks. He made them strong—his own because he thought it might get the cobwebs out of his brain and let him think more clearly, Vi's because she was watching and would complain if he made hers weaker than his own.

"Forgot to ask you, George. How's Luke?"

"Huh?" He'd forgotten his story of the original destination of his trip. Then he remembered. "Oh, fine. And L. A.'s just like it always was only more so. How was your stay in Santa Fe?"

"Wonderful, George." There was something about her expression that made him wonder how she meant that. She'd always liked Wayne Colby—and Madge Colby always took sleeping powders when she went to bed. But it didn't really matter; he didn't give a damn. And she was probably assuming that at least part of the purpose of *his* trip had been a bit of straying off the reservation.

Well, hadn't it been? He hadn't thought of Vi once, really, from the time he left her in Santa Fe until the time he got back; he'd thought only of another woman, one eight years dead. And did that make it better or worse?

Jenny. Had the trip laid her ghost? He knew all about her now, who she was and where she'd come from and why she had died and who had killed her and what had happened to him afterwards. He knew the whole thing now; he could start trying to forget it.

But who had stolen that letter—and in God's name, *why?*

He drank his drink and thought about it. Finally he had the answer; he'd last seen that letter the night when he'd found it and had been so terribly drunk. And it had been a find so important to him that he must have hidden it, not put it with the rest of Jenny's things, and then forgot about hiding it. Tomorrow, just to satisfy his curiosity, he'd hunt and find it. That's what *must* have happened. But what about the other evidences of a search—the drawer he himself had noticed, whatever it was Vi had noticed that made her think things had been moved? Well—it could have been that someone had been here but he'd been looking only for money or jewelry, and there hadn't been any money or jewelry around. Sure, that explained everything there was to explain.

He felt better, with that out of the way.

It didn't leave a loose end. He hated loose ends.

Maybe that was why he'd been so interested—almost obsessed—by the case of Jenny; at the first there'd been so *many* loose ends, so much that was unexplained. Maybe, now that he had all the answers, he could even get himself around to the point of view where he could write up the case after all. Hadn't he been rather ridiculous about that?

He finished his drink. Vi was putting fried eggs on the table so he didn't make another one just yet, although the first one had done him good.

They ate and he wiped dishes for her, what few dishes there were, because he wanted something to do. He made them another drink while she put them away.

"Vi—"

"What, George?"

"Nothing. Skip it." What had he been going to say? What *was* there to say? What had there ever been—in the last five years, anyway—to say between them?

"All right, George. Mind if I turn on the radio awhile?"

He shook his head. She went into the living room and he heard the click of the switch. He stepped out of the kitchen door, glass in hand, into the cool evening; it was just getting dark.

He wanted to take a walk—but he didn't want to take a walk, because he knew where he'd walk to, and it was meaningless for him to go there.

He thought, am I going crazy? *Really* crazy, not just a nervous breakdown or its aftermath?

He tried to look at it objectively; if this had happened to another man, and had been told to him coldly, objectively, he'd say that the other man was insane. But, from the inside, it looked different.

But why had it happened?

Because—well, because he'd been wide open for it, for one thing. Nature abhors a vacuum. And maybe, to some extent, contrast of his picture of Jenny with the reality of Vi? That may have been a factor. Poor stupid, uninteresting Vi, with her radio (he could hear it now, indistinguishable but gushing voices), with her need for candy and whisky and getting fat and sloppy physically as she was already fat and sloppy mentally, with her lackadaisical housekeeping and bad cooking and—well, above all perhaps her lack of interest in anything at all that could be a bond between them. She was getting more and more like—go ahead and think it; it's true—like a cow. But it's not a cow's fault that she's a cow, is it? He should remember that, always. And at least it was lucky, for her sake, that she now loved him no more than he loved her.

His glass was empty. He went back into the kitchen. The bottle that he'd opened was gone; Vi must have taken it into the next room with her.

The radio sounded blaring from here. "Where are you from, Mrs. Radzinski?" "Well, from Denver, really, but I've been living in Alamosa. That's where I came here from, I mean." "Alamosa? Beautiful little town, Mrs. Radzinski. To be from, I mean. I'm just kidding you, Mrs. Radzinski. I've never been there—but I'd like to go there some day. Now, Mrs. Radzinski—"

Weaver didn't want to go into the living room for his drink. He opened a new bottle instead and poured himself a big double drink so it would last awhile. He went outside again and the radio must have been turned louder in the meantime for he could hear the words now, not just the voices. He took his drink to the shed.

He got out the canvas from behind the stacked pictures. He unrolled it and looked and reached—and jerked his hand back. God damn it, he told himself; you're not a fetishist. Don't act like one. He rolled the canvas up again and put it back.

Where could he have hidden that letter? And what if he hadn't— He jerked his mind away from that possibility just as he'd jerked his hand away from the contents of the canvas. If the letter had been stolen, then the case wasn't closed because there was an unexplained factor.

But the case *was* closed.

He didn't like the light; he didn't like being in the shed. He turned out the light and went outdoors; he sat down on the step. He finished his drink and started for the kitchen to get another, then remembered he'd brought the new bottle with him and it was in the shed. He went back in and made himself another drink.

*You fool, are you going to get drunk again tonight? Wasn't night before last bad enough—so drunk you don't remember checking in at a hotel, so drunk that you remember something that didn't happen at all, that couldn't have happened because it doesn't make sense? But how did you imagine it? Maybe there had really been a big man with a badge behind his lapel and maybe he showed it to you just to shush you up and later your mind manufactured the rest as a dream while you were asleep in the hotel you don't remember going to. But not even a complete dream; you remember going to the cell, but you don't remember leaving it—and that's because your dream stopped there.*

He'd better stop drinking now, right now, because he was feeling it. And it was silly enough to get drunk ever, but to get blind and drunk two nights out of three—God, was he becoming an alcoholic?

But back there in the house Vi was probably getting drunk too.

Maybe he should—

No, he thought; it's purely animal when it's only that. And you're a little more than an animal, you hope. Better to have only dreams than so sordid a reality that two people want one another only when both of them are drunk.

He got up and started to walk.

There was a sliver of moonlight, just enough to see by when his eyes were accustomed to it. It was on a night like this, he thought, that Jenny was killed.

There was the cottonwood.

He couldn't make out the outlines of the shallow grave, not in this dim light, but he sat awhile under the big tree. He found himself dreaming the fantasy dream again—the dream in which he'd happened to stop in the bus depot that day eight years ago in Santa Fe, before he'd even met Vi, and happening to meet Jenny there and—and it was such an absurd fantasy because she wouldn't have paid any attention to him if he had been there, and why should she have?

He walked back to the house.

The radio was roaring. But it seemed to be between two stations, neither of them quite succeeding in drowning out the other, so he looked into the living room and Vi was asleep in the chair, her chin hanging—and showing the start of another chin below it. He looked at the level of the whisky in the bottle on the table beside her; she'd been putting it away even faster than he had. But then he'd walked to the shallow grave and that had taken time. "Bong, *bong, bong,*" said the radio; "This is KJA, your Albuquerque station. The time is nine o'clock. We bring you Wilson Randolph with the news. But first—Sun*shine* Bread! Sun*shine* Bread! Yes, folks, the bread that's *packed* with vitamins, the bread to ask for the next time you go to your grocer's. Sun*shine*—"

He got it turned off before he would have had to scream. The time announcement had penetrated, but it was so unbelievable that he looked at his wrist watch. The radio had been right; it was really only nine o'clock.

The silence sounded strange.

"Vi," he said, to break it. "Let me help you into bed, huh?"

She didn't answer, but she was partly conscious when he put his hands under her arms and lifted her out of the chair. She walked, staggeringly; he didn't have to carry her. He got her shoes and stockings off and opened the top of her dress. She started snoring the moment he put her on the bed. Weaver covered her up and closed the door so he wouldn't have to listen to her snoring. He went out into the other room and made himself another drink.

Nine o'clock. Oh Christ, only nine o'clock. And he wasn't sleepy. He'd slept late that morning in Santa Fe so he wasn't tired and he wasn't sleepy; it would be hours yet before he could even think about going to bed unless he wanted to lie awake and stare into darkness.

And how long now, already, had he been staring into darkness?

Try to read? God, it had been over a month since he'd been able to concentrate more than a few minutes at a time on reading.

Only nine o'clock.

Silence so deep that he heard the car coming a long way off and when it got near he went to the front window to look; with this the last house on the road it had to be coming here.

The car turned into the driveway. It parked behind his own.

A man got out of it and he switched off the car lights as though he intended to stay for a while. It wasn't Callahan; Weaver didn't recognize him.

Weaver wondered what the hell and then he decided he didn't care what the hell; he went to the door and opened it just as the man got there. He was a short but heavy-set man in a blue serge suit. He looked familiar, at close range; Weaver decided that he'd seen him a few times, probably around Taos.

"Mr. Weaver?"

"Yes. I'm Weaver."

"I'm Tom Grayson. Sheriff. Like to talk to you."

"Come in," Weaver said. He stepped back from the door. "Let's go out to the kitchen to talk, Sheriff. My wife's asleep in the bedroom and we'll be less likely to wake her if we talk out there."

Grayson knew his way to the kitchen.

"Drink, Sheriff?" Weaver discovered that he still had his own glass in his hand.

"Thanks, no. Not right now. Listen, Mr. Weaver, you got yourself in trouble, do you know that? I got you out. But I've got an explanation coming—and you've got some listening to do."

"Trouble?" Weaver stared at him.

"Day before yesterday. In Tucson."

"My God," Weaver said. It had happened, then—his arrest and release. "Sit down, Sheriff. And tell me what you're talking about. I mean—well, I was drunk in Tucson. I thought I remembered— But *why?* What did I do?"

"Nothing in Tucson. But you sure made an ass of yourself in Barton."

Weaver put his drink down carefully on the table. "Will you give it to me in words of one syllable, Sheriff? I don't get it at all."

"A Mrs. Albright phoned the police in Barton. She said a man who said his name was Weaver and who was driving a car with a Missouri license phoned her and then came to see her; he was drunk and acted—well, more than suspiciously; she thought he was insane. He told her that her daughter had been murdered by a madman with a knife—and that she thought, if his story was true, he must have been the murderer."

"My God," Weaver said. "I had that coming. Go on."

"The Barton police figured he'd maybe been other places, asking questions around, so they phoned a few places where he'd likely have gone. Especially the taverns, because she said he'd been drunk. And he had been at one of the taverns and had asked a lot of questions about Jenny Albright. He'd given the same name there and had said he came from Taos. He'd shown a hell of a lot of interest in a guy who'd dated Jenny and whom the bartender had seen later in Tucson. He'd sounded like maybe he was going to Tucson to look for the guy. Everything beginning to make sense to you, Mr. Weaver?"

Weaver said, "The mills of the gods grind slowly but they grind exceeding small."

"Huh?"

"Never mind, Sheriff. Go ahead."

"So the Barton police phoned Tucson, gave your description, and said they'd better pick you up for investigation. That was the middle of the evening; they found you in a tavern, drunk."

"They did indeed. Go on, Sheriff. And are you sure you won't have a drink?"

"No drink. I'm leading up to bawling the hell out of you Weaver, and I can't do that if I'm drinking your liquor. Are you sure you're sober enough now to get and remember what I'm saying?"

"I'll never forget it, Sheriff. Go ahead."

"Well, meanwhile, they phoned me in Taos—I mean the Barton police did—to find out if a guy named Weaver really came from here and what made him tick. And it was damn lucky for you that I already knew, from Callahan and Ellie Grant, what your interest in the deal was, so I was able to tell them you were all right; you were just writing up the murder for a magazine. And Barton phoned Tucson and the Tucson cops let you out of the cooler."

"Sheriff, I owe you a lot of thanks for that."

"Save them. I got to wondering, right after that call, how you'd found out that Jenny Ames—Jenny Albright—came from Barton. You couldn't have guessed it, and that meant you'd found evidence you weren't turning over to me—as you should have if it was anything new. So I came out here and looked around—legally, you understand; I had a warrant. I found that stuff wrapped in the canvas out in your shed; I looked around outdoors till I found out where you'd dug it up. That was smart of you, Weaver—I got to give you that much—to find that stuff he'd buried. But you ought to have come to me with it—especially that letter. I took it along, if you've missed it. You shouldn't have gone off on your own like that and tried to pull a fancy one."

"I suppose I shouldn't have," Weaver said. "I—well, it doesn't matter now. Nelson's dead, so the case is closed. Did you find that part of it out?"

"Sure, we had the same lead to Tucson you had; we followed it up the same way, only a bit later. Nelson's dead, all right."

He looked at Weaver, "Why'd you say a thing like that to Jenny's mother?"

Weaver dropped his eyes to his glass. "I'm not proud of that, Sheriff. I was a little drunk and—well, she needled me into it by telling me she didn't care what had happened to her daughter. Made me so mad I threw that at her without thinking."

He looked up. "And, Sheriff, I should have turned that stuff over to you, I admit; I guess it was just for my own ego that I wanted to follow through on it on my own. I'd have given you the dope before the article hit print, and full credit. I wasn't trying to chisel."

He thought, what the hell am I crawling for? This guy did me a favor by getting me out of trouble in Tucson, but I'd have got out anyway after they questioned me. And why am I lying about the article? I'm not going to write it.

"All right, Mr. Weaver." Grayson stood up. "But—well,

take my advice and don't write that article just yet."

Weaver stood, too; he looked at Grayson. "Okay, I'm not in any hurry to write it. But, out of curiosity, why not? All the facts are in, aren't they?"

They were; they had to be. Even the two loose ends he'd tried to keep from thinking about—the missing letter and what had happened to him in Tucson.

Grayson said, "Listen, Mr. Weaver, you think you're a detective or something just because you can write stories for magazines. You think you're smart. You think us ordinary officers don't know our ass from a hole in the ground. But that's where you're wrong. You haven't got sense enough to check little things, details, and we have."

Weaver frowned. "All right, what little things didn't I check?"

"You didn't bother to get a description in Barton, of this Jenny Albright. You didn't find out she was a blonde, not a brunette."

"You mean—" Weaver's mind reeled. "Are you kidding me, Sheriff—trying to tell me Jenny Albright wasn't Jenny Ames? My God, the letter, everything—"

"No, I don't mean that. It was Jenny Albright who came here under the name of Jenny Ames—and she'd dyed her hair along with changing her name, which is why Carlotta Evers and Pepe Sanchez saw her as a brunette. Sure, it was Jenny Ames who was here that night, the one he saw get chased out of the house into the dark. But—there's a but."

Weaver waited.

"But it wasn't, it couldn't have been Jenny Ames or Albright that was found in that shallow grave under the cottonwood. That girl, Weaver, was a real brunette, not a dye job. I checked back to the coroner's report of his examination and that's for sure. Besides, that body measured five feet five and Jenny's mother says she was five three exactly. Two inches difference is a hell of a lot. And other things."

Weaver shook his head to clear it. "All right, I'm stupid. I'm a horse's ass or anything you want to call me. But what's the score?"

"The score is that tomorrow I'm coming out here with two men. We're going over the whole area. We may find another shallow grave or two. Maybe it wasn't just one murder. Hell, the original Bluebeard didn't kill just one woman, did he? How do we know *how many* girls Nelson lured here to bring money to him, and then killed and buried out there somewhere? We know now there were two anyway, the girl that was in the grave out there, and Jenny.

"Or maybe he did kill only one, for all we're sure. Hell, for all we know Jenny Albright might have got away; she had a lead on him going out the door and maybe she outran him. Unless we find her body we don't even know she's dead. That's what I mean when I tell you to hold off on that article."

"But—but she *must* be dead, Sheriff, or she'd have gone—"

"To the police? When she thought she was wanted for embezzlement and knew that would come out if she told her story?"

The sheriff flipped a hand. "Be seeing you tomorrow." He walked toward the door and Weaver sank back in the chair. He reached for the whisky bottle and refilled his glass; some whisky slopped out on the table but he didn't even notice.

*Jenny might be alive. Why couldn't she have run faster than a man who, even then, had moderately advanced tuberculosis and whose stamina must have been low?*

*And if she was alive he'd find her.*

Sound of the motor of the sheriff's car starting. Weaver hurried to the door and out into the night, to the side of the car. "Sheriff, will you let me work with you on this? Help you from now on?"

"You didn't give us a lot of help, keeping that suitcase and the letter from us."

"I—I'm sorry about that. No more holding back, honest."

"Well—we'll see."

"I'm interested, Sheriff. Damned interested." *Jenny, if you're alive I'll find you.* "Listen, Sheriff, I want to be *sure* of one thing. The body that was found—it *couldn't* have been Jenny? I mean—"

"That much is for sure, Weaver. Even if she grew two inches and dyed her hair all over, it couldn't have been

Jenny. Jenny's mother says she's got a mole on her left hip; if there'd been a mole on the body, Doc Gomez would have made a note of it. That old boy was thorough."

Weaver turned and walked blindly into the house, into the kitchen. The sheriff's car drove off but Weaver didn't hear it.

Vi had a mole on her left hip.

Vi was five feet three and blonde. He'd met Vi three months after Jenny Ames had escaped from Charles Nelson. She'd been working as a waitress in Santa Fe, only seventy miles away on the main highway. She had no relatives. She'd been twenty-two.

Vi was Jenny. Jenny was Vi.

Santa Fe, the most likely place for her to have got a lift to, after she'd found her way back to the main highway that evening. The nearest town big enough to hide in, big enough to give her work.

He tried to pour himself a drink but this time his hands were shaking so he couldn't even hit the glass. He took a drink from the bottle.

He went to the bedroom door and opened it, looked and listened. That gross, sodden, stupid, snoring—

He braced himself against the doorjamb and made himself turn and go back into the kitchen.

*Jenny.*

He leaned against the table and reached again for the bottle. If he could only drink himself into a stupor quickly, *quickly*; it was the only way he could possibly keep his sanity, keep himself from—

"George."

Jenny stood in the doorway. Her eyes were bleary from sleep and drink, her face blotchy, her mousy hair snarled, her voice thick.

"George, was somebody here? And then you left the bedroom door open and the light—"

She'd come into the room as she was talking, but she stopped now, between him and the outer door, looking at him in bewilderment.

"George, what—?"

There was nothing he could do except what he *had* to do,

jerk open the drawer of the kitchen table and reach inside it—

*Sudden terror in her eyes, Jenny backed away from the knife, her hand groping behind her for the knob of the kitchen door. She was too frightened to scream and anyway there was no one to hear, no one but the man who came toward her with the knife—and he was mad, he must be mad. Her hand found the knob of the door and . . .*

## About the Author

Fredric Brown wrote 28 novels, 22 of which were crime novels. His short stories appeared in over a score of magazines, mostly detective and science fiction, and several have been adapted for television shows like "Alfred Hitchcock Presents," "Star Trek," and "The Outer Limits." Fredric Brown died in 1972 and, in an irony common to his generation of writers, has come into much critical acclaim since his death.